"Who?"

Sydney blinked up at her father. "What?"

"Who are you dating?"

Her gaze slid to the stranger, and she thought maybe white knights *did* ride to the rescue. It was worth a shot. What could happen? Even if this backfired, maybe her dad would get the message that she was serious about convincing him to back off.

"Him." She angled her head. "I'm going out with him."

Before her father could turn and look, she was on her way over to the man. Stopping in front of him, she looked up and said in a low voice, "I will forever be in your debt if you go with me on what's about to happen. It's a family thing." She put a fair amount of pleading into her tone and her expression. "I'm begging you. And I'll make it up to you. I swear."

**The Bachelors of Blackwater Lake:
They won't be single for long!**

Dear Reader,

"I have family..." That statement warms the heart, but we all know that relatives come with responsibilities as well as blessings.

Have you ever wondered how far you would go for someone you love? What you would do to see a family member find happiness?

That's the dilemma facing Sydney McKnight in *A Decent Proposal*. She never knew her own mother, who died giving birth to her. But a bit of guilt is just one of the reasons she asks a perfect stranger to pretend he's dating her.

Her father has been secretly going out with the mayor of Blackwater Lake and has found love again. It would be good news if he wasn't refusing to take the next step until his daughter is settled down, or at least seriously involved with a man. She tries to convince him she's got a boyfriend, but her dad isn't buying it. At that moment Burke Holden rides in to McKnight Automotive like a white knight to the rescue. Syd asks him to follow her lead, then implies she and Burke have been going out. In return she will give the good-looking guy a free oil change. A decent proposal, right? Things always seem simple at first, but there are inevitable complications.

This book is for all the readers who wanted to know if Sydney McKnight would be getting her story. Here you go! I hope it's worth the wait.

Happy reading!

Teresa Southwick

A Decent Proposal

Teresa Southwick

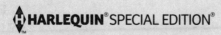

Recycling programs
for this product may
not exist in your area.

ISBN-13: 978-0-373-65878-7

A Decent Proposal

Printed in U.S.A.

www.Harlequin.com

Teresa Southwick lives with her husband in Las Vegas, the city that reinvents itself every day. An avid fan of romance novels, she is delighted to be living out her dream of writing for Harlequin.

Books by Teresa Southwick

Harlequin Special Edition

The Bachelors of Blackwater Lake

The Rancher Who Took Her In
One Night with the Boss
Finding Family...and Forever?

Montana Mavericks: 20 Years in the Saddle!

From Maverick to Daddy

Mercy Medical Montana

Her McKnight in Shining Armor
The Doctor's Dating Bargain

Montana Mavericks: Back in the Saddle

The Maverick's Christmas Homecoming

Montana Mavericks: The Texans are Coming!

Her Montana Christmas Groom

Men of Mercy Medical

The Doctor and the Single Mom
Holding Out for Doctor Perfect
To Have the Doctor's Baby
Cindy's Doctor Charming
The Surgeon's Favorite Nurse

Visit the Author Profile page at Harlequin.com for more titles.

To my nephew, C.J. Boyle. Your courage and determination inspire me every day. There's no question that you have a hero's heart.

Chapter One

Sydney McKnight knew there was no way a white knight would ride in on his stalwart steed and save her, but a girl could hope.

Needing a good save is what happens when first thing in the morning your father, who was also your boss, hits you with the "are you seeing anyone?" question. It was a sure bet this conversation wasn't headed anywhere she wanted to go.

Standing outside the office of McKnight Automotive, she glanced around for an escape, but short of making a run for it, there was no way out. Time to get the attention off herself and back where it belonged. On her father, who she and her brothers just found out had been seeing someone in secret. For months. And now Tom McKnight was looking to find out if his daughter would be in a committed relationship anytime soon so that he could take the next step in his own.

"Dad, you didn't have to sneak around and date. The boys are fine with it."

"It wasn't Alex and Ben that concerned me, Syd. It's you." He met her gaze and there was no looking away or mistaking his meaning. "I will always have a special place in my heart for your mother."

Complications from childbirth had caused her mother's death. Syd knew she wasn't to blame for it but that didn't stop a small stab of guilt. "For years everyone has been telling you to get on with your life, Dad. Now we know you did, a while ago. With Mayor Goodson. It's about darn time and I'm completely fine with it. Fly. Be free. Be happy."

Her father's expression tightened into a mask of stubborn resolve. "How can I be happy until I know your personal life is in order?"

That was code for having a man. What her father didn't get was that first you had to *want* a man messing up your personal life and Syd didn't. This wasn't the first time they'd had this conversation, but she was going to do her best to make it the last.

"Dad—" She stopped and took a deep breath, tapping into her well of patience, which at this point was hitting rock-bottom. "I know you want to protect me, make sure I'm okay. And it's really sweet, but I'm a big girl now."

"I know you are, honey, but I can't help worrying about you. Sue me. I want you to be settled, safe and happy." He ran his fingers through his thick silver hair. "Maybe it's about me being emotionally unavailable to you after your mom died."

Emotionally unavailable? "You've been watching TV talk shows again, haven't you?" she teased.

"Maybe." His grin was fleeting.

"There's nothing to make up for, Dad. I understand. Losing your wife was a shock. You're a terrific father.

The best. You did a great job. Alex, Ben and I turned out pretty awesome."

"You'll get no argument from me about that." His blue eyes twinkled with paternal pride. "The thing is, honey, your brothers are both married and have started their families."

And she was still very single, which translated to all alone. He didn't say it, but the implication hung in the silence between them.

Over her father's shoulder, Sydney saw an expensive, low-slung sports car growl to a crawl on Main Street in order to make the turn into McKnight Automotive. The beautiful, red, high-performance vehicle said something about the person driving it. For one thing, whoever it was didn't mind being noticed. A machine like that was an attention magnet. Her fingers itched to get a look at what was under the hood—of the car.

Focus, Sydney, she thought. "Alex and Ben were lucky to find their wives, Dad. You wouldn't want me to marry in haste then find out it was a mistake, would you?"

The sports car pulled into the driveway then roared past them and stopped under the covering that connected the business office and service bays of the garage. A dark tint on the windows prevented her from seeing who was behind the wheel, but she realized anticipation was swelling inside her to get a look at this person.

"Of course I don't want you to rush into marriage," her father said. "But I know how it feels to be alone. At least if I knew you were dating someone…"

"I date." Sort of.

"Anyone steady?"

If steady dating was the formula for a lasting relationship, she'd be married now. She'd had a boyfriend for years and the whole thing had blown up in her face. "Dad, don't worry about me. Just move on with your life. You deserve to be happy and I won't stand in your way."

"So, you're not dating," he said.

"Sure I am."

The sports-car driver got out and her heart actually skipped a beat, which had never happened to her before. The driver was a man. Aviator sunglasses hid his eyes, adding to his mystique, but she could see enough to know he wasn't a troll. He was thirtysomething and had dark hair. An expensive suit perfectly fit his tall frame, broad shoulders and narrow hips.

"Who?"

She blinked up at her father. "What?"

"Who are you dating?"

Her gaze slid to the stranger and she thought maybe white knights *did* ride to the rescue. It was worth a shot. What could happen? Even if this backfired, maybe her dad would get the message that she was serious about convincing him to back off.

"Him." She angled her head. "I'm going out with him."

Before her father could turn and look, she was on her way over to the man. Stopping in front of him she looked up and said in a low voice, "I will forever be in your debt if you go with me on what's about to happen. It's a family thing." She put a fair amount of pleading into her tone and her expression. "I'm begging you. And I'll make it up to you. I swear."

One corner of his mouth rose but with the sunglasses she couldn't see his expression. Her father joined them and there wasn't time for the stranger to respond.

"Sydney Marie McKnight, what in the world is going on? You've got some explaining to do."

"This is my dad, Tom McKnight." She slid her hand into the man's large palm and smiled up at him. "Dad, this is… This is the man I've been going out with." Dear God, she didn't know his name! She was holding his hand and didn't feel a wedding ring, so that was something.

The man she'd "been going out with" pushed the sunglasses to the top of his head. Amusement sparkled in his eyes. They were blue—a shade just on the other side of piercing and guaranteed to make a woman weak in the knees.

"Nice to meet you, sir." He held out his right hand. "Burke Holden."

Okay, then. The sports-car-driving, expensive-suit-wearing stranger didn't plan to rat her out just yet.

Her father shook the man's hand, but suspicion was written all over his face. "So you're going out with my daughter."

"That's what she tells me."

Very smooth, she thought. Quick, too. Fate would no doubt charge an exorbitant fee for putting a man with exactly the right skill set directly in her path. But that was a problem for another time.

"I haven't seen you around Blackwater Lake." Tom folded his arms over his chest.

"My company owns that property up on the mountain." It wasn't a direct response, just the insinuation that he'd been spending a lot of time here.

"Where the new resort is going to be."

"Yes, sir."

Syd liked the feel of her hand in the stranger's since the contact made it much easier to play this part. "You know better than anyone, Dad, that Mayor Goodson has worked hard to promote expansion in Blackwater Lake. She's determined to do it in a responsible, balanced way—not duplicating established businesses but attract new ones. And that will create the need for more services, jobs, build the tax base in a slow, steady, stable way. More people move to town and their cars need maintenance and repair."

"Part of the resort deal includes building a small regional airport," Burke explained. "There's no point in expanding anything without giving folks transportation choices to get here more easily."

"Makes sense." Tom nodded. "So you're not looking to put Blackwater Lake Lodge out of business? Because my daughter-in-law owns it."

Her family did actually, but Syd decided to keep that thought to herself. Camille Halliday McKnight had married her doctor brother, Ben. In the beginning, she'd had her doubts about the heiress but Cam was the sweetest, most down-to-earth filthy rich person Syd had ever met. And her brother was happy, which was the most important thing.

"No, sir. My company is interested in building condominiums with retail space below. A mixed-use development. The project is big enough to bring in revenue to existing local businesses. Workers will need lodging and food. It's a win for everyone."

"Maybe." Eyes narrowed, Tom looked down at her but directed the next question to Burke. "How long have you known my daughter?"

Oh, boy. Time to jump in and help. "Dad, have you ever met someone and right from the beginning you felt as if you'd known them your whole life?"

"No. And in case you're wondering, I noticed you didn't answer the question."

"Look, Dad—" The sound of the office phone ringing interrupted.

"I'll get it. But we're not finished with this, Sydney." Her father gave her a *dad* look then headed inside to answer the call.

When they were alone, Syd blew out a long breath. "Thanks for going along, Mr. Holden—"

"Burke, please. After all, we're going out. I'm the guy

you met and felt as if you'd known all your life." His voice was teasing, his smile incredibly attractive. "So, do you want to tell me what that was all about?"

"Not really, but I owe you an explanation." She gathered her thoughts. "Here goes. Twenty-five words or less. You're obviously a busy man."

"Yes, but this is the most intriguing thing that's ever happened to me."

"I doubt that, but okay. If you say so." A man who looked like him probably had intriguing encounters with women every day. "My dad has been a widower for a long time, actually since the day I was born."

"Your mother died in childbirth?" He looked shocked.

"Yes. And for years everyone has been telling him to get a life, but he wouldn't. Recently my older brother dropped by the house unexpectedly and found Dad in a compromising situation with the mayor. I can't say more or the idea of him with a woman—doing stuff in bed— will be burned in my brain and require years of therapy. Long story short, for close to a year they've been secretly dating."

"Way to go, Tom." There was an admiring expression on Burke's face when he glanced at the office doorway.

She laughed, then grew serious. "He's found love again."

"Good for him. But what does that have to do with you?"

"He wants to ask the mayor to marry him but won't get on with it because of me. Both of my brothers have gone all white-picket-fence and settled down. Marriage, babies, the whole deal. Dad wants the same for me. Or at least to know I'm dating and moving somewhere in the vicinity of settling down."

"I see."

"You probably think I'm crazy, and who could blame

you? You just had the bad luck to arrive as I was being grilled like raw hamburger. I'd just told him a big fat lie about going out with someone. He wanted to know who and there you were. I'm terribly sorry to have dragged you into the madcap McKnight family like this. But I really do appreciate what you did."

"Like I said, very intriguing." He slid his hands into his pockets. "What are you going to do now?"

"Nothing. He's met you. That gives him a visual and he'll propose to Loretta and they'll get married."

"Won't you need a date for the wedding?"

"You'll be conveniently out of town." She smiled at him. "After all, you're a very busy man. And at just the right time I'll share the news that you and I have broken up."

"Hmm." The corner of his mouth quirked up. "Will I have dumped you?"

She laughed. "Not after you were so understanding. The least I can do is take the blame. Or it will just be one of those things that didn't work out. No one's fault."

"But I'll be heartbroken," he protested.

"Something tells me you'll find someone to make it better."

"I've heard of speed dating," he said, shaking his head, "but this is the fastest relationship I've ever had."

"Aren't you glad you were in the right place at the right time?" Wow, he really was smooth. Looks, charm and wit made him a triple threat. The single ladies of Blackwater Lake would be forming a line, but Syd wouldn't be in it. She wasn't interested in complicating her life. "And that reminds me—what brings you to McKnight Automotive?"

"Oil change."

"Okay. It's on the house." When he opened his mouth to protest, she said, "I insist. I told you I'd make it worth your while."

"All right. Thanks."

"You helped me out of a jam so it's the least I can do. Want to wait for it? We have a comfortable lounge with coffee, soft drinks and snacks."

"No, someone is picking me up." At that moment, a big, black SUV pulled into the driveway and parked behind the sports car. "As a matter of fact, there's my ride."

"Give me a number where I can reach you when it's ready," she said.

Burke pulled a business card out of his wallet and handed it over. "Thanks, Sydney Marie McKnight."

"No—thank you."

Burke smiled, then walked to the passenger side of the car and got in. The vehicle drove out of the lot and she watched until the taillights disappeared down the street.

Tom came out of the office. "Someone needs a tow out on Lakeview Drive. I'll take care of it."

"Okay."

"Burke seems like a nice young man."

"He is." It wasn't every guy who would get sucked into a scenario like that and just go with it. Points to the handsome stranger.

"I want the four of us to go out to dinner."

"Four?" Her stomach dropped.

"Loretta and me. You and Burke."

"I don't know, Dad. He's…busy," she said lamely.

"Everyone is but he's managed to find the time to date you." Her father's voice had an edge of suspicion. "And everyone has to eat. So we'll double-date. Unless you're lying to your old man."

It was hard not to flinch. There probably wasn't a place in hell low enough for her. Still, she was doing the wrong thing for the right reason and that had to count for something.

"Really, Dad. You raised me better than that." This bad was all on her.

She cared about her father's happiness. He'd spent so many years being sad and alone and he wasn't getting any younger. He deserved happiness and she wouldn't be the one who stood in his way. If she had to scheme to make sure it happened, by God she would.

The guy had seemed really easygoing and she was giving him a free oil change. What could it hurt to ask?

"I'll check with Burke and see what I can set up."

"I'll call again tomorrow, son." Burke held the cell phone to his ear, not sure why he was prolonging this.

"Okay." His child's familiar, formal tone was the polar opposite of enthusiastic.

"If you need anything, you know how to get in touch."

"Yeah." There was a long silence, then Liam said, "I have homework."

"Right." He probably wasn't the only father on the planet whose kid would rather do homework than talk to him, but it sure felt that way. "I love you. 'Bye, son."

"'Bye."

Feeling guilty and inadequate, Burke hit the end-call button on his cell phone. He never knew what to say to his son and heard in the kid's voice how much he was let down whenever they talked. Not calling would save them both the ordeal of an awkward conversation, but unlike his own father he wouldn't take the easy way out. So he would be in touch every day while he was away from home.

His ex-wife was no better. During divorce negotiations she'd put up zero fight when he wanted physical custody. Now she lived in Paris and he had the best housekeeper in Chicago. Most of the time that made it okay for him not to be there. At least that's what he told himself. Today he didn't quite buy it. Meeting Sydney McKnight and her father, Tom, might account for that.

He found himself envying their obviously close relationship. She had gone above and beyond to convince her dad to move on with his life. That was loyalty, a happy by-product of a father who'd been a positive influence on his daughter. Burke couldn't help wondering if twenty years from now Liam would go to that much trouble for him.

Normally he didn't feel lonely on a business trip but today was different. In a lot of ways. He was sitting on a stool in the Blackwater Lake Lodge bar. There were a couple of businessmen, two women who'd stopped in for a drink after work and several couples having a predinner cocktail. He was nursing a beer while he waited for Sydney to personally deliver his car.

She'd contacted him and offered; now he found himself looking forward to seeing her again. Stereotyping probably described his attitude, but he'd never expected to see a woman so beautiful, sexy and smart working in a garage.

And speaking of beautiful women, there was one who'd just come around the corner from the lobby and waved when she saw him. Her last name was McKnight, too, but Camille was married to Sydney's brother, Ben. Burke considered her a friend and she knew about his bad-relationship karma. That's probably why she'd never told him about her husband's sister.

She stopped beside him and they hugged. "Hi."

"Hello, Mrs. McKnight. Marriage looks good on you." In spite of his dark mood it was impossible not to smile in the presence of a woman glowing the way this one was. "You're positively radiant."

"Thank you, kind sir." She put her hand on his arm. "Love does that to a person. You should try it sometime."

"Been there, done that. It didn't work out."

She wrinkled her nose. "That wasn't love. Brenda was selfish and self-absorbed. Probably still is."

"Almost certainly," he agreed.

The Holden and Halliday families had been friends for

years and partners in various business ventures, including a small stake in the project he was here to work on.

"How's Liam?" she asked. "He's how old now?"

"Eight. Getting big."

"You must miss him when you have to be away on business," Cam said.

Burke nodded ruefully. "It's not easy."

"The time goes by so quickly." She sighed. "My little girl is growing so fast."

"That's right. You're a mom now." He grinned. "Motherhood agrees with you. How old is…" He didn't know the child's name and shrugged apologetically.

"Amanda—Ben and I call her Mandy. She's fifteen months. You have to meet her while you're here."

"I'd like that—"

A flash of red coming around the corner caught his eye and he did a double take. The blazer belonged to Sydney McKnight and she wore it over a white silk blouse tucked into jeans that fit her like a second skin. High heels made her legs look a lot longer than he knew they were. She was pretty in her work clothes and stunning in the sophisticated outfit.

Camille followed his gaze. "Ah, my sister-in-law. Wow, she really cleans up well. But then she always dresses like a fashion model when she's not at the garage. She looks fabulous."

Burke had noticed. Earlier her hair had been pulled into a sassy ponytail but now it fell like dark silk past her shoulders. Layers framed her small face and highlighted her big, brown eyes. She could be in *Car and Driver* magazine or grace the cover of *Glamour* or *Cosmopolitan*.

Sydney saw the two of them and looked surprised for a moment before heading in their direction. She stopped in front of them.

"Cam, it's nice to see you." She leaned in for a quick

hug. Then she looked at him. "So, you've met my sister-in-law?"

"Actually we've known each other for years," he explained. "As a matter of fact, the Hallidays have invested in my resort."

Sydney blinked. "You own the development company?"

"With my cousin, yes." Her surprised expression was genuine. "Why?"

"You just said your company owned the land."

"We do," he said.

"I just thought you were on the payroll, not the guy who signed the paychecks for everyone." Syd glanced at Cam, who nodded a confirmation. "Be sure to share with my father that you know this guy. He had your back today."

"Oh?" Cam said.

"That's right," Burke agreed. "I brought my car into the garage for an oil change and he gave me the third degree about the new project followed by a subtle warning that it better not put the lodge out of business."

"I'll be sure and tell Tom not to worry. He's so thoughtful. I'm so happy he finally found someone, and the mayor is a good woman." Cam looked first at Burke, then her gaze rested on Sydney. "Is this a coincidence you two meeting here?"

Sydney dangled a ring of keys on the end of her finger. "Like Burke said, he brought his car in for an oil change and I'm delivering it now."

"And I appreciate the service."

"Happy to oblige."

"So everyone is happy." Cam grinned at both of them then released a regretful sigh as she checked the watch on her wrist. "I'd love to stay and chat but I really need to get home to Ben and the baby."

"Give them both a hug for me," Sydney said.

"I will." She looked at Burke. "We'll put a date on the

calendar soon for dinner so you can meet my husband and Mandy."

"I look forward to it," he said.

Cam smiled, then turned and walked out of the bar, leaving him alone with Sydney. Their gazes locked and he felt something squeeze tight inside him. He wasn't sure what it meant but knew she'd completed her errand and would leave if he didn't come up with a reason for her to stay. And he really wanted her to stay.

"Can I buy you a drink?" he asked. "It's the least I can do. What with you going out of your way to bring my car back here to the lodge."

"I'd like that." She gracefully slid onto the bar stool beside his. Without hesitation she said, "Chardonnay, please."

Burke signaled the bartender and asked her to open the best white she had. He toyed with the empty beer bottle in front of him. "I can't decide if this delivery system of yours is good customer service or you just wanted to drive my car."

"Both. And for the record it's a really nice car," she said, grinning. Then the amusement faded and she couldn't quite meet his gaze, which was different from the uniquely direct woman he'd met this morning.

"You look very chic."

She glanced down. "Thanks. Are you surprised?"

"Because you make your living working on cars?" He thought for a moment and decided to be completely honest. "You're a beautiful woman, Sydney. I was surprised from the very first moment I saw you this morning."

"What a lovely thing to say. And I appreciate it." Her smile was a little shy, but also…nervous? "Because there's something I'd like to ask. A really big favor—"

"Your drinks." The twentysomething blonde waitress put down a small, square napkin, a wineglass and another beer in front of him. She picked up the empty bottle and said, "Let me know if you need anything else."

"Will do. Thanks," Burke said. He held up his beer. "To new friends."

Sydney touched her glass to his bottle. "Friends."

She was definitely nervous about something. Then her words sank in. Favor. Something to ask. "What's up?"

"This is harder than I thought."

"Just spit it out," he advised. "That's usually best."

She took a long drink of Chardonnay, then set the glass down and looked him straight in the eye. "Nothing ventured…"

"Now I'm really curious." His impression of her from their first meeting was of a confident, forthright woman so this hesitation struck him as out of character. "The worst that can happen is I'll say no."

"Actually that's not the worst. And saying yes would not be the smartest answer."

"Come on, Syd." Shortening her name came easily and naturally, but he didn't have time to wonder why that was. "Just tell me what's on your mind."

"Okay." She took a deep breath. "I really need you to go out with me on a date."

Chapter Two

"You probably think I'm a gold-digging stalker."

"Why would I?" Burke was more curious and intrigued than anything else.

"Today at the garage you said your company owns the property on the hill that's going to be developed. As in the way people say my company is doing a hostile take-over but I just work for them and do what I'm told. As in a highly placed executive or something. It didn't cross my mind that you *owned* the company. I had no idea you were in the same league with Camille's family. The one where billionaires come to play."

"Surprise."

Sitting on the bar stool, she angled her body toward him. "And I hit on you!"

"It happens."

"I just bet it does." There was humor in her dark eyes. Usually getting hit on turned him off. Sydney McKnight had the opposite effect. Color him shocked by this unex-pected reaction to a small-town girl.

"Seriously, Burke, I wasn't hitting on you. Not exactly. Not you...you. Any single man who was in the right age group and happened to drive up at that moment would have done just as well."

"Way to let the air out of my ego balloon." He took a sip of his beer.

"I'm not being mean. Just honest."

"I like that about you, the honesty part." And so many other things. Like the graceful arch of her dark eyebrows. The way her full lips curved up as if she found some-thing secretly amusing. And the intelligence sparkling in her eyes.

"The thing is, Burke—and I don't mean this in an offensive way—but what you think of me isn't my big-gest problem."

He rested his elbow on the edge of the bar and half turned toward her. "That would imply that you might be in a bit of a predicament."

"That would be accurate."

"I see."

When he moved his leg, her knee bumped his thigh and it felt oddly intimate for a bar setting. More people had wandered in for drinks but it seemed as if he and Sydney were alone. He found himself wishing they were.

"Did I hurt your feelings, when I insinuated that your opinion of me isn't important? That certainly wasn't my intention."

"Not at all. Do I look like my feelings are hurt?"

She sipped her white wine and studied him. "I don't know you well enough to make that determination. There was just an odd expression on your face."

Hmm, she was very perceptive. He'd have to watch

himself around her. "I assure you my feelings are just fine. So tell me about your problem."

"Well it's like this. My father is a little skeptical about our relationship."

Burke laughed. "Can you blame him? It does feel suspiciously like a scenario from a TV sitcom."

"I don't know what came over me." She sighed and shook her head. "You have no reason to believe this but I swear I've never done anything like that in my life. Accosting a strange man and pulling him into my situation."

"*Accost* is sort of a strong word."

She grinned. "I mean this in the nicest possible way, but you're very good at going with the flow. Lying without really telling an untruth."

"Thank you, I think."

"Seriously, it was very generous of you not to rat me out on the spot."

"I'm a generous guy."

"Why didn't you, by the way? Tell my dad I was crazy, I mean."

That was a very good question and one he didn't really have an answer for. "Chalk it up to curiosity about what you were up to."

She nodded, then looked down and toyed with her cocktail napkin. "The thing is…" Her gaze lifted, meeting his. "Dad wants proof that we're actually dating."

"You mean like photographs with a time and date stamp? Movie-ticket stubs? Eyewitness accounts?"

"If only." She sighed. "He wants to go out to dinner. A double date. You and me. Dad and Loretta—Mayor Goodson." She held up a hand to stop any protest and went on quickly. "Just think about it. I swear this isn't a scheme to snag a wealthy husband, but I can see where you might think that."

Normally that's exactly what he would think, followed

quickly by the thought that it was a wasted effort. He would never get married again. Once was enough, and he'd learned he wasn't a very good husband. The best thing to come out of the relationship was his son, but he wasn't a very good father, either.

"I appreciate you hearing me out, Burke." She finished the wine in her glass. "I love my father very much and would do anything to see that he's happy."

"He's lucky to have a daughter like you."

Frustration tightened her delicate features. "If he was really lucky, he'd have a daughter who was settled and he wouldn't have to worry about her. I think I'm a big disappointment to him."

"I sincerely doubt that. And take it from me—settling down with the wrong person is a bigger problem than being alone."

"Sounds like the voice of experience talking." She studied him for a moment, then said, "But you don't have to tell me about it. That's personal, and on a need-to-know basis. I don't need to know."

"There's not much to tell and if you really wanted the information it would be easy to do an online search." He tapped his fingers on the bar. "Most people go into marriage believing it's the right thing and I'm no exception. It wasn't right. Things didn't work and we got a divorce. Completely amicable and civilized. Including dealing with the custody of our son."

"You have a child." It wasn't a question.

"Yes." His fingers tightened on his beer bottle.

When he didn't say more, she nodded. "You know, I have this ridiculous urge to say I'm sorry. But it sounds like you're okay with everything."

"I am." Except for the fact that his son would always carry the scar of coming from a broken home and a mother who showed no interest in him.

"Anyway, think it over. My cell number is on the card I gave you." She picked up her small purse from the bar and slid the strap onto her shoulder. "Give me a call and let me know if you're in for round two of this covert operation."

"You're leaving?"

"Yes. I've taken up enough of your time."

No, she hadn't taken up nearly enough, he thought. "But you dropped off my car. How are you going to get home?"

"I'll call Dad. Thanks for listening, Burke." She slid to the edge of the bar chair, getting ready to go.

"Wait." He put his hand over hers to stop her. "I have a question."

"Okay. Shoot." Her gaze lowered to where he was touching her, but she didn't pull away.

"I can't help thinking that every unattached guy in town would want to go out with you. Wouldn't you be better off with one of them?"

"I had one of them." Her eyes darkened for a moment before she smiled, an expression with just the barest hint of bitterness. "It didn't work out. Ancient history." She slid off the stool. "The fact is, you're the guy who had the bad luck to pull into McKnight Auto Repair at just that moment. I shot my mouth off and you went along with it. Now you're either in or you're not."

"And what if I'm not?"

"My father will not propose to the woman he loves and live happily ever after. If you're okay with ruining his life..." A teasing smile turned up the corners of her full mouth. "No guilt."

"Right. Guilt doesn't motivate me." Unless Liam was the one using it. "But count me in."

"Really?" A bright smile lit up her whole face. "You're sure?"

"Yes. I would love to have dinner with your father and the mayor. And you, of course."

"Oh, Burke. I could kiss you."

"Feel free," he said generously.

"Right. You don't really mean that."

Yes, he really did. "I'm happy to help."

"I don't know why you're willing to go along with this but I'm grateful. Seriously, thanks."

"You're welcome."

Oddly enough it had been an easy decision. The simple answer was that he'd agreed because she asked and he wanted to see her again. Granted, he could have asked her out, but he'd already have had a black mark against him because of turning down her request. Now she owed him.

She leaned against the bar, a thoughtful look on her face. "I've never done anything like this before, but I know my father. He'll ask questions. In fact he already did. We're going to need a cover story. How we met. How long we've been dating. That sort of thing."

"It makes sense to be prepared."

"So we should get together soon and discuss it."

"What about right now?" he suggested.

Her eyes widened. "You don't waste time, do you?"

"No time like the present. Have you already had dinner?"

She shook her head. "Why?"

"Do you have a date?" If not, there was a very real possibility that she'd changed into the red blazer, skinny jeans and heels just for him. Probably wanted to look her best while making her case. Still, he really hoped she wasn't meeting another guy.

She gave him an ironic look. "Seriously? If I was going out with someone, I wouldn't have asked you to participate in this crazy scheme."

"Crazy? I don't know, it's a decent proposal." He shrugged. "So you're free. Have dinner with me. What about the restaurant here at the lodge? It's pretty good."

"The best in town." But she shook her head. "Too intimate."

So she didn't want to be alone with him. "Oh?"

"Something more public. People should see us together." She snapped her fingers. "The Grizzly Bear Diner would be perfect."

"I know the place. Both charming. And romantic."

"You're either being a smart-ass or a snob."

"Heaven forbid."

"You haven't been there yet?" she asked.

"No, I have."

He signaled the bartender and when she handed the bill to him, he took care of it. Then he settled his hand at the small of her back and said, "Let the adventure begin."

Sydney sat in the passenger seat beside Burke as he expertly drove the expensive sports car from Blackwater Lake Lodge to the Grizzly Bear Diner on Main Street. She wasn't sure what she itched to get her hands on more—the steering wheel of the hot car, again, or the man holding it. She'd said she would have hit on any single man who happened to drive into McKnight's Automotive just then, but, wow, she couldn't imagine anyone more perfect.

She would be lying if she said him having money wasn't cool. But after talking in the bar, she was much more intrigued by his wit and sense of humor. There was a glint in his blue eyes that could be about mischief or something more sizzling and she didn't particularly care which.

"Here we are." He pulled the car to a stop right in front of the diner.

"That's unusual."

"What?"

She met his gaze. "Getting a spot out front. I guess since this is a weeknight and school just started up after the summer, it must be a slow night."

"Are you disappointed?"

"Not really," she said. "But more people would help spread the word to my dad that we're an item."

He exited the driver's side and came around to open her door. Offering his hand to help her out, he said, "It doesn't look very crowded but we'll work with what we've got. Maximize resources."

"Okay."

When he locked the car and took her hand in his she was instantly stricken with a bad case of the tingles—from head to toe. Every nerve was on high alert and threatening to light up all her feminine hormones.

The buzz died when they walked inside and Syd recognized the new hostess, who just happened to be an old friend. Well, former friend. More of a frenemy. Violet Walker—actually it was Stewart now. The woman looked up from behind the wooden stand with the sign that said Please Wait To Be Seated. The automatic "welcome to the diner" smile froze on her face.

Still holding Syd's hand, Burke must have felt a reaction because he asked, "Something wrong?"

Other than the fact that she'd come face-to-face for the first time in years with her former bestie who'd stolen and married the man Syd had expected would propose to her?

"No," she answered in a tight voice. "Everything's just peachy."

They walked closer to the other woman and Syd said, "Hello, Violet."

"Sydney. Hi." The familiar blue eyes were filled with guilt.

"I didn't know you—and Charlie—were back."

"Surprise."

Syd was pretty much at her tolerance limit for surprises tonight. That didn't stop her from noticing that Violet's thick brunette hair was shorter, cut in an edgy bob that was very flattering.

"You look great, Syd."

"So do you."

That was no automatic response. Violet was curvier and it looked good on her. She'd always been too thin. If anything she was even prettier now than when she'd begged forgiveness for falling in love with Sydney's boyfriend.

Violet looked at the man still holding Syd's hand. "Nice to see you again, Mr. Holden."

"It's Burke, remember?" His tone hinted that he'd said it more than once. But he'd said he knew the place, which probably meant he'd been here a few times.

"Right. You've been in here enough to know everyone's name." The other woman's smile was strained. "Two for dinner?"

"Yes. A booth in the back if you have it."

"Right this way."

There weren't many people in the place, but all of them were long-time residents of Blackwater Lake who knew what had happened between the former best friends. As they walked clear to the back of the diner, Syd felt all of them looking, wondering, and decided a slow night had been a blessing in disguise. Not that news of her and Burke wouldn't spread, but it was easier to see Violet again in front of a smaller crowd.

Violet stopped at an empty booth. "How's this?"

"Perfect," Burke responded.

"Enjoy your dinner." The words were professional and matched the smile on her face.

When she was gone and they were seated across the table from each other, Burke asked, "So, want to tell me what that was all about?"

"Not really, no."

He opened his mouth to ask more, but the diner owner

walked over. Michelle Crawford, a brunette whose hair was streaked with silver, was somewhere in her fifties. Her brown eyes were filled with concern.

"Hi, Syd. Burke, it's good to see you again." She settled a look on Syd. "You didn't know Violet and Charlie moved back, did you? And this is the first time you've seen her since…" She lowered her voice. "You know. I could tell by the expression on your face."

Any hope that no one had noticed her reaction went right out the window. "No," she said, "I didn't know they were back."

"Oh, honey—" Michelle touched her shoulder. "Your dad should have warned you."

"He knows?" The words were automatic, but obviously he did. "Probably a heads-up slipped his mind. But it's fine, Michelle. Been a long time. Don't give it another thought."

"All right, honey. Glad you're okay." She smiled, then pointed to the menus stacked behind the napkin holder. "I'll let you look over the choices and be back in a few minutes to take your orders."

When she was gone, Burke's eyebrows drew together. "Whether you want to or not, it's probably best that you bring me up to speed on your ancient history."

"Are you going to tell me about yours?" He was divorced and had a son. She was curious about that.

"As it pertains to our agreement, yes. Like you said— need-to-know basis. But Blackwater Lake is your turf. And what happened to you is probably something you would tell a boyfriend."

Before Syd could respond, an older couple walked over to the table. Tillie Newman and her husband, Pete, were friends of her father and brought their Ford F-150 truck in for an oil change every six months, like clockwork.

"Hi, you two." Syd looked at them, trying to figure

out how to deflect what she knew was coming. "Mr. and Mrs. Newman, have you met Burke Holden? His company is building the resort we've heard so much about." She glanced at him. "Burke, this is Tillie and Pete Newman."

"Nice to meet you." He stood and shook hands with them.

"Same here. Welcome to Blackwater Lake." Tillie's brown eyes brimmed with sympathy when she looked at Syd. "Sorry to interrupt, but we saw you and Violet. You could just cut the awkwardness with a knife. I just had to make sure you're all right, sweetheart."

"I am. That's all water under the bridge. Or over the dam. Whatever the saying is. No need to be concerned about me."

Tillie looked relieved. "I'm glad. We always liked Violet and Charlie. Real nice to see them move back where they both grew up. It had to be hard, what happened between you."

It had been incredibly hard at the time, Syd recalled. "Time heals all."

"There's my girl." Tillie smiled and said, "We'll leave you two alone now. Come along, Pete."

"Take care, Syd. Truck's due for that oil change soon," the older man said.

"See you then." She lifted her hand in farewell and watched their backs for as long as she could. When procrastinating was no longer possible, she met Burke's curious gaze. "So you're probably jumping to all kinds of conclusions."

"It doesn't take a world-class detective to connect the dots."

Syd nodded. "The Charlie they mentioned is a guy I dated in high school and college. I thought he was moving toward a marriage proposal. It turned out that he was— just not to me."

"Violet?" he ventured.

"Yes. She was my best friend since first grade."

"That must have been tough." He reached over and covered her hand with his own. "He's the one you mentioned. The one who didn't work out."

"Yup." She glanced away for a moment. "This is the first time I've seen her since all that went down."

"And?"

She knew he was asking how she was feeling about it all. "I was shocked to see her since my father failed to share the news of her return. But…"

"What?" he asked.

"I was so hurt and angry back then." She shrugged. "It's all gone. It really is okay that they're back. Their parents are here and I'm sure happy to have them close by again."

"So you're sure you don't want to postpone our planning session for another time and place yet to be determined?"

"I'm sure," she said adamantly. "And even if I wasn't, no way I would leave. McKnights are made of sterner stuff than that."

"Okay, then." He grabbed the menus and handed her one. "What do you recommend?"

"You tell me. Seems you've been here enough that you're on a first-name basis with people."

"It's a small town." His look was ironic. "And there aren't many dining choices. I've been here a little over a month and have made the rounds. More than once."

"Is this where you pitch the new resort as a solution to our cuisine choice issues?"

"No. This is where I remind you that even if I'd only been here once, I'd stick out like a fly in milk. I'm… memorable."

"True." It was hard to believe she hadn't met him before today. Not only because he was right about it being a small town. But she also felt as if they'd known each other much longer. She grinned. "As far as this menu—I like the She Bear burger."

He looked down and read the description and raised an eyebrow. "Jalapeño? Mushrooms, bacon and Swiss cheese?"

"I hear disapproval in your tone. Don't knock it until you've tried it."

He was studying the choices and a sort of tender look came over him. "Liam—my son—would like this place."

"You're looking at the Baby Bear combo." When he nodded she said, "You miss him, don't you?"

"Yeah." There was an expression in his eyes that said he didn't want to elaborate. "I think I'll have the Papa Bear combo."

When they closed their menus it was a sign to Michelle and she was back to take their orders. "I'll have these out in a few minutes."

After the diner owner was gone, Burke rested his forearms on the edge of the table and met her gaze. "So what questions do you think your father will ask?"

"For starters he'll want to know where and how we met. Just so you know, he won't go for an online dating service."

"Oh?"

Syd settled the paper napkin over her knees then straightened the knife, fork and spoon that had been wrapped up inside it. "He's an old-fashioned guy and doesn't believe 'the machines,' as he calls them, should be a part of meeting your soul mate."

"Okay. So it has to be a plausible face-to-face encounter." He linked his fingers. "Where do you hang out that our paths could have crossed?"

"Bar None, the bar where locals go. Potter's Ice Cream Parlor and The Harvest Café. Here at the diner. But word would have gotten out if we even talked for five minutes under the watchful eye of Michelle Crawford."

She looked around the diner, with its pictures of grizzly bears on the walls. At the front of the place there was a counter lined with swivel stools. The back half had scattered tables in the center of the room and booths lining the perimeter.

"Okay. Any ideas?" he asked.

"There's a multiscreen movie theater at the mall about forty-five minutes away."

"I've been there," he said.

"Do you like movies?"

"Yes. Besides that it's something a person can do alone and not get pity stares."

"Oh?"

He nodded. "I've noticed that when you eat by yourself people give you weird looks."

She realized that he was lonely and it took considerable effort to keep pity out of the look she gave him. It was her sense that he wouldn't appreciate the sentiment.

"So, Mr. Gazillionaire Real-Estate Developer, is the crown too tight? Are the jewels too heavy?"

One corner of his mouth curved up. "I'm not sure what that means."

"Just that you have buckets of money, expensive clothes, a car that most people drool over and you're concerned about the way people look at you?"

He shifted on the seat. "When you put it like that…the correct response would be no."

"That's what I thought." The glint was back in his eyes and she much preferred that. "So we could have met at the movies."

"Is that plausible for you?"

"I go alone all the time. It's relaxing after a marathon

shopping spree. For the record no one pities a solo shopper."

"Good to know." He nodded. "I'm guessing we'll need to explore explanations for why no one has seen us around town together."

"That one is easy." She leaned forward. "People in this town talk and we just wanted to keep it quiet. Just for us."

"Very romantic," he commented. "That works."

"Sure does. It's the explanation I got from my dad about why he kept his romance with Mayor Goodson under wraps. A lot longer than what you and I are talking about." She was still irked about his secrecy. This small charade with Burke might be a little bit about payback. And her comment that she was made of sterner stuff wasn't just hot air. She could have handled the news about his new relationship. "I'm too old for him to give me the 'do as I say, not as I do' line."

They discussed things and tossed questions back and forth until he held up his hands in surrender. "I feel as if I should be taking notes."

"You're right." She nodded. "Kiss rule."

"Excuse me?" One eyebrow rose questioningly. The look in his blue eyes turned a little sharper, a little sexier and a lot interested.

"*K-I-S-S.* Keep it simple, stupid."

"Ah." His gaze never left hers and the intensity level escalated.

"You were thinking something else?"

"Yes. And before you judge, remember this is logical."

"Enlighten me," she said drily.

"We may be forced into kissing. After all this—you and me as a couple—needs to be convincing."

Their burgers were delivered, breaking the sensuous spell. But all through dinner she had a hard time not staring at his mouth and wondering what his lips would feel like against her own. Was he a good kisser? She would put money on it.

Sydney found she was looking forward to "dating" Burke Holden and was intrigued at the prospect of kissing him.

Chapter Three

Two days after his strategy session with Sydney at the diner, Burke was sitting in the five-star restaurant at Blackwater Lake Lodge nursing a Scotch while waiting for her to join him with her father and the mayor. He was watching when Tom McKnight and Mayor Loretta Goodson walked in with a stunning, dark-haired woman wearing a little black dress. He recognized Sydney, but…holy shoot, it felt as if all the blood drained from his head and proceeded to points south of his belt. Fortunately muscle memory and manners took over so he was able to not embarrass himself and politely stand up as the trio approached.

Burke held out his hand to the older man and said, "It's good to see you again, sir."

"Likewise." Tom McKnight looked at the older woman beside him. "I think you already know Loretta?"

"We've had a number of meetings about the resort."

Burke shook her hand. "Madam Mayor, it's always a pleasure."

"I couldn't agree more, Burke." Loretta Goodson was a very attractive brunette and probably looked a whole lot younger than she actually was. All those meetings had proved that she was a tough negotiator who cared deeply about her town.

Syd smiled up at him. "Hi."

"Hi, yourself." He slid his arm loosely around her waist and bent to kiss her cheek. It wasn't the way he really wanted to kiss her for the first time, but appropriate for the situation. "Why don't we all sit."

"Good idea," Syd agreed.

The Fireside Restaurant service was impeccable and tonight was no exception. When the newcomers were seated, their waiter appeared to take drink orders, then promised to give them time before bringing over dinner menus.

"So, where did you two meet?" Tom didn't waste any time and had come right to the point.

Since the man was looking directly at him Burke fielded the question. "I'm something of a movie buff and when you're alone in a new town it's an entertaining place to kill a couple of hours."

"Syd likes movies, too." Fortunately her dad jumped to the implied conclusion. "But how is it you managed to keep secret the fact that you're seeing my daughter?"

"Come on, Dad," Syd admonished. "Isn't that a little like the pot calling the kettle black?"

"She has a point, Tom." Loretta's voice was quiet but firm. "We've been seeing each other for months. I know some of that was about protecting your children, but part of it was about keeping it just for us."

Burke looked at Syd who had an "I told you so" expression in her eyes. She'd definitely called that one.

The waiter brought their drinks, then came back with

menus when Burke gave him the signal. It was quiet at the table as everyone scrutinized the choices. He'd eaten here enough in the last few weeks to know what he wanted and would much rather have looked Sydney over. Tonight she'd pulled her hair off her face and back into a messy side bun, leaving her neck bare.

The urge to taste her skin just below her ear was very powerful and if the two of them were alone at a quiet table in the shadows, that's exactly what he would have done. The strong attraction he felt certainly helped to pull off the pretense of having an interest in her because it really wasn't a pretense.

He *was* interested.

When everyone was ready the waiter took their orders. As it happened, he and Sydney chose almost the same things. Fireside chopped salad, although she asked for it without blue cheese crumbles. Filet mignon, medium rare. Baked potato with sour cream, butter and chives on the side.

Syd gave him a look that was half saucy, half surprised. "You have good taste."

Tom's expression was still just this side of skeptical. "He hasn't brought you here before?"

"If he had, you would have known about it," his daughter reminded him. "Camille owns the place and is normally the soul of discretion when it comes to lodge guests. But family is a different matter entirely. She couldn't keep something like that from you."

"It's a good quality in a daughter-in-law." Tom leveled his gaze at Burke as if to say he'd better have equally good qualities.

"Toast." Loretta raised her glass of white wine. "To new beginnings and happy endings."

They all touched glasses then took a sip of their respective drinks. When he glanced at Syd, he noticed a guilty look on her face and questioned whether or not he would have recognized the expression if he wasn't in on this scheme of hers. It made him wonder about her growing up and who better to ask than her father.

"What was Sydney like when she was a little girl?"

The older man looked fondly at his daughter. "Stubborn. Determined to get her way. She didn't like dolls the way other little girls did, but that could be from having two older brothers." He grinned. "Of course, she had me wrapped around her little finger."

"You did a wonderful job raising her," Burke said and sincerely meant it.

"She raised herself."

Loretta shook her head and put her hand on his arm. "You don't give yourself nearly enough credit, Tom. I know how difficult that time was for you, suddenly losing your wife. Then you were thrown into the deep end of the pool with two young boys and an infant daughter to bring up by yourself, while running your own business. The McKnight kids didn't get to be successful adults without your guidance and being a steady role model for them."

"You're making me blush." He took Loretta's hand in his own and smiled tenderly at her.

"I could go on torturing you," she teased. "I know how you hate to have anyone singing your praises."

Burke watched the older couple banter and laugh, comfortable with each other and clearly in love. From what Syd had said and Loretta had just corroborated, he knew Tom McKnight had had a rough go of it and had been alone for a long time. Burke realized how much his daughter loved him. She wanted him to be happy and was going above and beyond so that he would take the next step in his relationship.

A small deception. Wrong thing; right reason. Theirs was a close and loving relationship forged by his being there day after day. It made Burke feel even more guilty than usual about the long stretches of time he spent away from his own son.

Dinner was really pleasant and surprisingly interrogation-free, right up until the dessert menus arrived.

Syd looked hers over. "I'd love some coffee and just a few bites of something sweet."

"Order it and just eat what you want," Burke suggested.

"That's so wasteful," she protested. "And, unlike my leftover steak, dessert can be pretty unappetizing the next day."

"We could split something."

"I'm not sure we could agree and I don't want you to compromise for me."

"I'd be happy to compromise for you," he said. "But what if we do agree?"

"Okay. Tell me what your favorite is." She tilted her head to the side, making her neck look longer and even more tempting.

Quite possibly a nibble right at the juncture of her neck and shoulder could be his favorite, but that wasn't what she'd meant. So he answered honestly. "The mile-high chocolate cake. I've been all over the world and it's the best I've ever tasted. Anywhere."

"What do you know?" She smiled as if he'd given her the moon. "That just happens to be my all-time favorite, too."

"Then the deal is sealed."

When the waiter returned they ordered coffee all-around, one piece of cake and four forks. It was definitely enough for the whole table to share.

"Speaking of deals…are you two getting serious?" Tom glanced at Burke, then at Sydney.

"Dad!" She looked mortified. "Inappropriate."

"Not for a father," he insisted.

"Are you asking me what my intentions are?" Burke questioned.

"Sounds old-fashioned when you put it like that, but I guess that is what I'm asking."

This potential line of inquiry hadn't come up in their planning session. He looked at Sydney, wondering if she wanted to tackle that one, but she still looked shocked and speechless.

"Well, sir, for now we're taking things slow. Just getting to know each other. We both agree that's the best idea. Then we'll see what happens."

Tom mulled it over, then nodded. "Seems wise to do that."

Burke had to conclude that they'd passed the first hurdle. He'd done his best to answer everything honestly and still keep his word to Syd. But he realized that he liked her a lot and that was another topic they hadn't talked about. What if he actually wanted to date her?

In fact, tonight was their first official date and he was seriously considering taking things to the next level.

Sydney watched Burke charge the dinner-for-four to his room at the lodge and she was incredibly appreciative of the gesture. He and her father had done the masculine tug-of-war over the check that men always do, but Burke, as they said, was younger and faster. Although thanks had been expressed, she made a mental note to thank him again for his generosity the next time she saw him. And offer to split the bill with him.

The four of them stood and walked toward the restaurant exit, her father and Loretta in the lead. Burke leaned over and whispered close to her ear, "How do you think we did?"

It was difficult to form a reply, what with her unexpected breathlessness at his nearness. But she managed to recover. "We did pretty well," she admitted. "Loretta jumping in for backup was unexpected, but certainly strengthened the narrative we were promoting."

"Good. Apparently I played my part adequately, then."

"*Adequate* sets a very low bar for what you did. Your act was perfect."

Before she could say more, the couple in front of them stopped and waited. They were standing by the rustic stone fireplace in the lodge lobby with the registration desk nearby. Leather sofa and chairs formed a comfortable conversation area.

Tom extended his hand. "Burke, thanks again for dinner. I look forward to getting to know you better."

"Same here, sir." He looked at the mayor. "I believe we have a meeting this week."

She nodded. "We need to discuss local concerns about the resort."

"I'll be there to answer any and all questions." He didn't look the least bit concerned and his superior confidence was incredibly attractive.

"Are you ready to go, Syd?" her dad asked.

"You're leaving?" Burke put his hand at the small of her back.

"I rode into town with Dad and Loretta. So…" She shrugged.

"Stay for a nightcap." His eyes had just the right amount of intensity for a smitten man who didn't want to say goodnight yet. "I'll drive you home."

She wanted to protest that this wasn't part of the plan, but that would blow their cover for sure. "You must be tired after a long day. I don't want you to go out of your way."

"If I can spend more time with you, driving you home is not going out of my way." Now a definite challenge joined the intensity in his eyes.

Syd wasn't sure what game he was playing and was

wary of jumping in with her "come and get me" high heels. She'd picked this particular dress on purpose, knowing it was a little dangerous. The point had been to prove that she'd been dressing for a man's approval. This was an inconvenient time to realize it had done the job maybe a bit too well. When push came to shove she really had no choice.

She gave him her most brilliant smile and said, "I would love to stay. You don't mind, do you, Dad?"

"Of course not. As long as you make it to work on time in the morning."

She kissed his cheek while her own was flushed with the implication that she'd spend the night with Burke. "I won't be late tonight."

"But don't wait up," Burke said. "When Syd and I start talking, we lose track of time."

"Take good care of my girl." Her dad had that protective expression on his face.

"I will, sir. Good night."

When the older couple was gone, Burke took her hand and tucked it into the bend of his elbow before turning toward the lodge bar, where she'd first met him to propose this unlikely collaboration. Somehow the situation had slipped from her control and having a drink could further fuzzy her faculties on top of what her attraction to him did. Instinct was telling her she should stay sharp.

She looked up at Burke. "What about a walk instead?"

"In those shoes?" He took one step back and the corners of his mouth curved into a smile as he leisurely studied the four-inch pumps and her legs, all the way to where the hem of the dress stopped above her knees.

She shivered at the male approval clearly etched on his face. "I'm tough. Have you ever heard that Ginger Rogers did everything Fred Astaire did, only backwards and in heels?"

"I have actually. But I'm not quite sure what your point is since we're not dancing."

Says who? she thought.

"I'm not quite sure I had one," she admitted. "But as you probably know, there's a lighted walking path on the lodge grounds with benches here and there. If my feet can't take it, we can stop."

"A walk sounds good. It's a beautiful evening."

Burke put his fingers over hers, trapping her hand on his arm as they walked out the rear exit. To anyone observing them, they were a couple. Body language to support the story.

The evening air was cool, but not cold. As they strolled slowly down the cement path she noticed the moon peeking through the pine trees scattered over the grassy area.

"Did you know there was a full moon tonight?" she asked.

"No." He looked up. "But now that you mention it, this one is more beautiful than it is in Chicago."

"It occurs to me that the stage is perfectly set for romance. It's just a darn shame this is all going to waste on us."

"How do you mean?"

"We're just playing at it."

"That's the rumor," he answered mysteriously.

"And speaking of starting rumors…" She'd intended to express her gratitude for dinner the next time she saw him but hadn't realized she'd be alone with him quite so soon. But now was as good a time as any. "I just wanted to tell you how much I appreciate what you're doing for my dad. I didn't expect you to buy dinner tonight and I appreciate that so much. If you'd like I can reimburse you—"

"Of course not. Why would you think that?"

"I didn't mean to offend you. And I don't want to take

advantage of you. You're doing me a favor so I feel as if I should take the financial responsibility."

"No." He shook his head. "For so many reasons. But I sincerely meant what I said about it being my pleasure. I like your father. And he's a lucky man. Loretta is a wonderful woman. So I'm happy to give their happy ending a nudge."

How sweet was that?

She leaned into him just a little. "And I mean it when I say how appreciative I am for your participation." She thought about his moves from the moment he stared at her when she walked in, the kiss on the cheek, meaningful glances through dinner. Meeting his gaze, she said, "You're very good at this. The pretending, I mean. Should I be worried?"

"I'm getting whiplash. You went from appreciative to worried in a nanosecond."

"Don't get me wrong. I'm thankful for your talent but it makes me think you have practice."

"No." He laughed. "Just chalk it up to negotiating skills put to another purpose. I pay attention to details. I'm results-oriented and logistics are my strong suit."

"Well, you're playing your part to the hilt. That's really unexpected."

"Call me an overachiever." He stopped suddenly and looked down at her, something dark and exciting drifting into his eyes. "But consider this—did it ever occur to you that I'm not playing?"

She wasn't able to completely absorb the meaning of his words before he lowered his mouth to hers. The touch was soft and sweet. Seeking and seductive. His hand moved over her back, fingers brushing the bare skin. Shivers slid up and down her spine and her nerve endings started to dance. Heat balled in her belly when he put his arm around her waist and settled her more firmly against him.

It wasn't supposed to happen, but she kissed him back. She couldn't stop herself, didn't want to. Had she unknowingly given off vibes? Somehow let him know how attractive she found him? Whatever the reason, she was enjoying the heck out of this.

When he pulled back and looked at her, she could hear and see that his breathing was unsteady. She would have taken a great deal of satisfaction from that fact except hers was ragged, too. That wasn't good.

They stared at each other for several moments and she knew she had to say something. *Keep it light,* she thought. "That was a nice touch. Like I said, acting is your strong suit. But I'm surprised that you kissed me."

"The fact that you're a beautiful woman doesn't explain my motivation?"

Oh, how she wanted to be flattered, but it wasn't wise to go there. "It would, except that you've been seen with some of the world's most beautiful women."

"But none of them can keep the engine in my car purring like a kitten. And I don't mean that as a double entendre. You are a rare, unusual and special woman."

"Thank you." With every fiber of her being she wanted to believe that. "But remember we have to keep our eye on the ball. There are lofty goals at stake."

"It's never far from my mind."

"Good. Then you understand when I say that you can't be kissing me for no reason."

"Maybe I had one." He indicated the light just beside them that made their every move visible to the people milling around the lodge patio not far away. A member of the staff was straightening the outdoor furniture.

"So we could be seen. It's what a man dating a woman would do."

How silly was she to be even the tiniest bit disappointed

to learn that he didn't mean it? Later she would give herself a stern talking-to about how ridiculous her reaction was.

"Yes. And speaking of dating, we have to plan our next move. Your father's remark about looking forward to getting to know me better was his way of letting us know he's watching."

"I got that, too."

And she got something else from tonight. A warning that her control regarding Burke Holden was nothing but an illusion. He was a strong man, a powerful man accustomed to getting his own way. She'd dated guys and broken up with them and never looked back, but she had a sneaking suspicion that this could be different.

That didn't make her happy, but unfortunately she was stuck.

Chapter Four

On his way to the county buildings on the other side of Blackwater Lake, Burke drove past McKnight Auto and glanced over. Several cars were lined up waiting for service orders to be written up, but there was no sign of Sydney. He hadn't realized how much he'd hoped for a glimpse of her until he didn't get one. If she hadn't approached him with her unorthodox proposal, would he have asked her out?

On his part the attraction had been instantaneous so there was a better-than-even chance he would have. But after dinner with her father and the mayor the other night, it was crystal clear that if he'd followed his usual pattern of avoiding a woman he would have missed something... exciting? Special? Life-changing?

Maybe all of the above. But whatever happened, this *thing* could never be permanent. When it came to his personal life, *permanent* and *forever* weren't part of the vocabulary.

He turned left onto Mountain Street and drove a couple of blocks. The city and county government offices were on the right. He knew where the mayor's office was, having been there several times, and the construction-permits office was somewhere under the same roof.

He parked in the rear lot and walked through the heavy glass doors into the lobby. There was a directory on the wall and Burke saw that the building inspector's office number was located on the second floor. There was an elevator, but he found the stairs and headed up. Too many hours behind a desk could add weight to his midsection. He worked out daily at the lodge fitness center but never missed an opportunity to move more.

When he was home, Liam frequently asked him to play ball, any kind. Baseball, football, soccer. Too often Burke had to say no because of work commitments. He wished he could delegate a lot of details and be home more, but he'd tried that a few times and there was no one he trusted enough. Things got missed, delays resulted and when that happened it cost the company millions. Burke was building an already successful business with his cousin Sloan and someday it would be Liam's. He felt an obligation to leave it more profitable than he'd found it.

Burke located the office and went inside. There was a waiting area with a couch, chairs and a coffee table. A high desk was situated on the left and he walked over. A blonde woman somewhere in her late thirties or early forties was standing there.

"Hi. I'm Burke Holden."

"Sally Gardiner," she said, introducing herself. "I've heard about you."

"Really?" He in no way meant to flirt, but what was a guy supposed to say to that? Just be friendly. "I hope it was positive."

"You're the fella who's building that new resort up on

the mountain. You've got a flashy red sports car. And you had dinner with Sydney McKnight and her dad and the mayor at the Fireside the other night."

"News travels fast. And it's all true," he said.

"Generally stories being passed around town are factual and details aren't made up or exaggerated." She grinned. "Folks here in Blackwater Lake take pride in the integrity of our rumor mill."

"Good to know," he said.

"If anything, whoever's doing the telling plays down personal opinion. But you're even more handsome than I heard."

"Thank you. I'd hate to disappoint."

"So," she said, "are you and Sydney an item?"

In a way, he thought, but not how she meant. "Well…"

"Sorry. I'm nosy. But the thing is, folks are going to ask me. It'll be all over town that you were in here today." She shrugged.

"An item?" Burke thought for a moment. "Not unless you define an item as a man and woman who are getting to know each other."

"Hmm." It seemed as if she was the tiniest bit disappointed in the answer. "Okay, then. What is it I can do for you today, Mr. Holden?"

"Burke, please. You'll probably be seeing a lot of me around here." He smiled pleasantly, but there was no response from the clerk. "I'm here to look into building permits for the resort."

"You'll need to speak with the building department supervisor."

"That would be great. Is he free?"

"I'll check for you. Have a seat."

"Thanks."

Burke did as asked but had hoped to be shown in without having to wait. There was a lot to do back at the office and he had a scheduled call with his cousin soon. After ten minutes he began to look at his watch. Probably he should have called ahead to make an appointment. He didn't want to be perceived as presumptuous. That little detail would spread like a wind-driven wildfire and not make his work life in this small town easier.

Just when he was wondering whether or not to leave a message that he would call and schedule a time, Sally walked back behind the counter.

"Sorry I took so long, Burke. Had to update John on some things. He'll see you now."

Burke had seen John Donnelly, Building Supervisor, stenciled on the door to this office. "Thank you."

"Follow me. Through there." She pointed to the door separating the waiting area from the back offices.

Sally led him down the hall to the last office, which was probably the biggest. The door was open and she poked her head in. "John, this is the fella I was telling you about."

"Thanks, Sally." The man was in his late fifties, with gray hair and brown eyes. He was a little over six feet tall because they were eye-to-eye when he stood and held out his hand. "John Donnelly. Nice to meet you, Mr. Holden."

"Burke."

"Okay." He indicated the two chairs in front of a desk where construction plans were unrolled for further scrutiny. In the corners of the room, similar rolls were standing up in stacks, probably blueprints waiting for approval. "Have a seat, Burke."

"Thanks."

"What can I do for you?"

"I wanted to introduce myself. As you probably know, I'm in charge of building the resort up on the mountain. It's my job to facilitate construction, cross the *t*'s and dot the *i*'s. In my experience, the process of doing that is much smoother after I get to know who I'll be working with."

John, cool and assessing, leaned back in his desk chair. "I can see that."

"It would also be helpful to know what paperwork the county requires. Every one is a little different."

"Sure." The other man nodded.

"I've researched codes and zoning restrictions for Blackwater Lake but wanted to find out from the guy in charge if I have the latest information."

"I can help you with that."

"It would speed things along to know how many copies of the building plans and site plans you require. How much detail we need to add. Make sure you don't have to ask for more documentation." Burke looked at the man, who was nodding his agreement.

"That would sure help us out at this end," he admitted.

"Mayor Goodson assured me that the length of time required and the permit application process is shorter and less intense than a city like Chicago, Los Angeles or New York. Simply because here there's not the large volume of requests."

"True enough. But we keep busy."

"I have no doubt. The thing is, delays can be costly and time-consuming." Stuff that needlessly kept him away from home. And Liam. "I'd like to avoid that if possible."

"I can sure understand that." John leaned forward and rested his elbows on the desk. "And here's where I'm coming from, Burke. It's come to my attention that you're seeing Sydney McKnight."

"We've met," Burke said cautiously. The man's pleasant tone didn't change, but there was something uncompromising in his dark eyes. "Sir, I don't mean to be critical here. And I'm aware that things are different in a small town. But I'm a little confused about how that information is relevant to my getting construction and electrical permits issued in a timely fashion."

John pointed to a picture on his desk, one of several and nearly obscured by the unrolled paperwork. It was a photo of this man with his arm affectionately thrown across Syd's shoulders. Both were smiling. "Sydney is my niece."

Burke did his best not to show surprise. If the last name had been the same, he'd have been better prepared. This guy must be her deceased mother's brother. "I see."

"Maybe you do. Maybe not. It's not clear from what I hear whether or not you're dating my niece, but you should know that I've been extraprotective of her since the day she was born. So I'd prefer that she's a happy camper. That girl and my brother-in-law have been through a lot. I'd sure hate to see anyone do anything to hurt her." He hesitated a moment, letting the words sink in. "And whatever the mayor told you about a short waiting period for plan approval could be a little off. If you get my drift."

Burke definitely got it. The drift was clear. Don't do Sydney wrong or the permits could be delayed, costing him time and money.

He stood and met the other man's gaze. "I assure you that Sydney is safe with me."

"Sure hope so, son."

Burke shook the man's hand, left the office, nodded to Sally behind the desk, then walked into the hall and back down the stairs the way he'd come. This was an aspect of small-town life that he hadn't taken into account. Since his philosophy was not to get deeply involved with a woman, it hadn't occurred to him there was a potential conflict of interest if he did.

Still, he was pretty sure he'd told Syd's uncle the truth about her being safe with him. She wasn't looking to get serious and had volunteered to handle the details about them breaking up. Considering that, she should be able to pull off convincing everyone that she wasn't hurt by their relationship.

But any ideas Burke had of taking things to the next level with her would be best ignored. Personal risks weren't his style and factoring in the business complications made taking any chances too costly.

Still, he was committed to helping convince Syd's father they were a couple. That would make her happy and now he had business reasons for keeping her that way.

After rotating the tires, Syd looked at the underside of the 2012 Chevrolet sport utility vehicle up on the hydraulic lift. Always a good idea to make sure the frame was solid. The customer had said the ride wasn't as smooth as it could be. Part of the reason could be that Blackwater Lake was surrounded by rural area. Critters large and small crossed the roads whenever they felt the need and mostly at inconvenient times.

She didn't like thinking about that, but stuff turned up and finding it here at the shop was in her job description, so she looked and fortunately didn't see anything wrong. She would change the oil, then check the fuel injection system.

There were footsteps on the cement floor behind her. A man's footsteps in dress shoes, not boots or sneakers. Burke Holden.

Could be someone else, but she had a feeling it wasn't. Just thinking his name made her heart beat a little faster. She took a deep breath then turned to face him. "Hi."

"Hi, yourself."

"I'm guessing you didn't see the sign."

One corner of his mouth quirked up. "You mean the one about customers not being allowed in the service area?"

"That would be the one."

"It's a liability issue and I don't plan on having an accident, let alone filing a lawsuit against your business."

"Good to know."

He moved closer and pulled her into his arms, then lowered his mouth to hers. The sudden and unexpected intimacy sucked the air from her lungs and started her pulse racing. His lips were soft, so soft, and she felt herself sinking into the kiss in spite of the warning her brain was trying to send that she shouldn't respond.

He cupped the side of her face in his palm and brushed his thumb over her cheek, caressing, mesmerizing, tempting. The sound of a tricked-out truck roaring by on the street brought her to her senses, reminding her where she was.

She pulled back, hoping he wouldn't see that his kiss had affected her, made her tremble from head to toe. Brushing her dirty hands over her equally dirty work shirt and pants, she said, "I'm greasy. It's going to get all over those expensive clothes you're wearing."

He glanced down at his slacks and sports shirt and shrugged. "A devoted boyfriend doesn't care about things like that."

Speaking in the third person was a dead giveaway that he wasn't talking about himself. And for some reason that kiss had felt a lot like a giant "take that," as if he was trying to make a point to someone. "Why did you kiss me?"

"Your father's watching."

"How do you know?"

"I stopped in the office. He told me where to find you and warned me about customers in the service bay."

Syd peeked past him and saw that it was true. Tom McKnight was looking at them through the window of his office. It was so tempting to wave, but she held back. Make it look real and natural, she reminded herself. The man's future happiness was at stake.

She looked up at Burke. "I have to say again that you're very good at role-playing."

"It's a gift." His face had faux humility all over it.

"I didn't expect to see you here." But she was happy he'd stopped by, a thought that was something to rationalize later.

"I just met your uncle."

"Oh?"

He nodded. "I went to the county building services office about permits for the resort. Turns out he handles that sort of thing."

In the brief time she'd known Burke Holden, Syd had grown accustomed to his easygoing manner. It was missing in action at the moment.

"And?" she asked.

"Several things, actually." He smiled but there was no amusement in his eyes. "Sally Gardiner wanted to know if we're an item."

So the rumor mill was already grinding out information. It was good when a plan came together. "Don't keep me in suspense. What did you tell her?"

"That you and I are in the process of getting acquainted. She would have to make the determination about whether or not we're item-worthy."

"Good answer."

"Thank you."

"What else happened?" she asked. He'd said there were several things.

"Your uncle John warned me that if I hurt you the process for obtaining building permits would be significantly longer than I'd been led to believe."

"Did he actually say that in so many words?"

"Not exactly. It was more of a general implication."

So he had more skin in the game now. That's why he'd kissed her as if there was something at stake. "I'm sorry, Burke—"

"It would have been helpful if I'd known you were related to the man in charge of signing off on building permits."

She heard the annoyance in his voice and chalked it up to him not liking surprises. Couldn't blame the man for that. They weren't her favorite thing, either.

"I'm sorry, but I didn't know you were going to see him."

"I need permits before breaking ground on this project. That's a given."

Now she was starting to get annoyed. Syd put a hand on her hip and met his gaze. "I'm a mechanic, not a builder. It's not my job to know how that process works and I can't read your mind. If you'd mentioned it, I'd have passed on the information of a family connection." She took a deep breath. "I asked you to do me a favor and I'm grateful for your help. But if this is going to impact your business in a negative way feel free to back out. I will explain to Uncle John that this is my fault."

He stared at her for a moment, then smiled, chasing away most of the tension. "I think we just had our first fight."

Syd wanted to stay irritated but couldn't manage to maintain it. She laughed. "Who won?"

"I think it was a draw."

"Seriously though, how macho and protective was my uncle?"

"On a scale of one to ten?" He thought for a moment. "About a twelve. Firm but friendly."

"Uncle John isn't a mean, vindictive man. And he's extraordinarily professional. His integrity is impeccable. I'm sure he would never use his position of authority to settle a score. And I would never let it go that far."

"I believe you, Syd." He dragged his fingers through his hair. "But I need to hedge my bets. We've put a lot of time and money into materials, delivery, manpower and schedules. There's built-in flexibility for unexpected delays, but too many could be a big problem."

"I'll talk to him. Don't worry," she said. "He's really a sweetheart."

"Maybe, but the boundaries he set for his niece's boyfriend were quite clear." One corner of his mouth lifted. "And I'd rather wait before you talk with him and possibly jeopardize the plan."

"So you still want to go through with it?" She wouldn't blame him in the least if he backed out of the whole thing.

"Not only do I want to see it through, it's quite possible the number of official dates we agreed on won't be enough to convince him that I didn't have nefarious intentions such as leading you on."

"Are you talking about my dad or Uncle John?"

"Both."

"That's really generous of you, Burke." She shook her head. "But I really feel awful about this and it's not what you signed on for. I had no idea this could end up being a professional problem for you. I was only thinking about helping my dad."

"As far as potential business problems are concerned, let's cross that bridge if and when it becomes necessary. For now we act as if spending time together isn't a hardship."

It wasn't a hardship and she wasn't acting. "If it's a problem for you, hanging out with me, I mean—"

"Not at all." He took her hand and linked their fingers. "In fact it's interesting. Going through the 'getting to know you' stage on the way to 'being an item' phase of our relationship with everyone watching is…different."

"Really?" She was pretty sure the words were sincere, but figured the doubts creeping in were normal under the circumstances.

"Really. The thing is, what you asked me to do is way beyond what most daughters would do. I have to conclude that you'd do anything for someone you love. Any man would be lucky to be that someone. And it makes you quite a unique and intriguing woman."

"That's nice of you to say."

"It's not just words, Syd. I truly mean it." He grinned.

"Well...thank you." She didn't know what to make of that comment or the intensity of the gaze he settled on her. Somehow, the line was starting to blur between what constituted acting like a man who was interested and what was real. And the probability was that his motivation for doing this was to avoid business problems.

"And now, just in case your father is still watching..."

He leaned down and kissed her again. Just a quick brush of lips. The gesture a smitten man would make when he was saying goodbye to the woman with whom he was smitten. After pulling back, he moved in again for one more brief touch of his mouth to hers, as if he was reluctant to say goodbye.

"I have to go. I'll call you later."

"Okay."

She watched him walk away and was more confused than calmed by this visit.

The feel of her hand in his had felt warm and wonderful. She liked kissing him, too, which was fortunate because it was an aspect of playing the part she'd asked him to play.

The downside was that it felt too real. Falling for the man she'd pulled into her scheme wasn't part of the plan. She'd gotten him into this mess and now he was playing his part to the hilt so his resort project wouldn't be delayed.

Something about the way this was all changing made *her* want to back out. But she was doing this for her father and Tom McKnight hadn't raised a quitter.

Chapter Five

"Are you sure you want to go to this park dedication?" Sydney asked.

"Yes." It had been Burke's idea and they were on their way there now.

He looked at her sitting in the passenger seat of his car and had the absurd thought that she looked really good there. Her dark hair was long and loose, sexy and silky. A yellow, thin-strapped tank top left her shoulders bare and denim shorts hugged her hips in the nicest way possible. "It's a beautiful day. The sun is out. Sky is blue. And I've been told that this perfect weather won't last much longer."

"Who told you that?"

Actually her old friend Violet had mentioned it when he'd gone to the Grizzly Bear for lunch one day.

"People in the diner who have lived here." He glanced over and saw her mouth curve up, an indication that a sassy remark was coming his way.

"Do you believe everything strangers tell you?"

"As a matter of fact, I've grown quite close to some of the regulars at the Grizzly Bear Diner. That tends to happen when a guy is away from home and eating all his meals in restaurants."

"I'm guessing that's supposed to make me take pity and invite you over for a home-cooked meal?"

Burke was looking at the road ahead and couldn't see her expression, but heard the teasing in her voice. "Is it working?"

"We could make it one of our mutually agreed upon designated dates."

"Yeah."

He should be glad the terms of her proposal were clearly spelled out. The added pressure of a delay in building permits should have made him grateful that this didn't start out complicated.

But it was going in that direction. Ever since the day he'd stopped by the garage and told her about the conversation with her uncle, he'd gotten the distinct impression that Syd was putting him off. He'd asked her to dinner one night and got a vague response about having other plans. She declined an invitation to a movie with the excuse of an emergency job that required overtime at the garage.

There were notices all over town about the grand opening of the new park and all the planned activities to celebrate it. This morning he'd called at the last minute and before he could ask her out, she'd said she was going. He'd informed her that he was, too, and said he would come by her house in an hour to get her. Before she could wiggle out of it, he hung up. Now here they were, almost to the park that was located two blocks south of the square in the center of town.

He pulled into the newly paved parking lot and found a space between freshly painted white lines. A large banner was strung between two pine trees and proclaimed the grand opening of Blackwater Lake Park. Newly seeded grass was roped off, but cement paths led to a children's play area with multiple configurations of climbing apparatus, slides and swings. It was set on a hard foam foundation to make unanticipated landings a little more forgiving.

Burke felt a pang when he thought how much Liam would enjoy this, but he wasn't here. His son was following his usual routine at home and Burke hated that they were separated even though he believed stability was the most favorable option. Being a single dad, he always felt conflicted about what was in his son's best interest.

"It's awfully quiet over there," Syd said. "Either you hate this date with me, or the park has triggered some unhappy suppressed childhood memories."

He looked at her and his smile was forced. "I was just thinking how much my son would like this park."

"So he's got a thing for the outdoors?"

"He's a boy." Burke shrugged.

"Right. Enough said." She was studying him closely. "You really miss him, don't you?"

"Yeah, I do." She'd noticed his mood when he'd taken her to the diner for dinner. And the longer he and his son were apart, the more he could feel the emotional distance between them growing. Daily phone calls were unsatisfying. Infrequent trips home weren't enough to build a strong bond.

"You'll be here awhile, right? Why don't you have him with you? Unless his mother objects."

Burke hadn't told her much about his ex-wife and didn't really want to now so he ignored her comment. "When I got here in August I thought about having him here with me, at least for a few weeks until school started. But he doesn't know anyone and I'm working long hours."

"There are ways to deal—"

"What do you say we put the serious stuff on hold and go have some fun?" he suggested.

"That's code and it means you really don't want to talk about this." She stared at him for several moments, then nodded and opened her door. "Okay. Sounds like a plan. Dad's already here. He had to show up early to help organize. When I texted and told him we were coming, he answered that he'd grabbed a table and there was room for us."

They exited the car and headed up the walkway to the area designated for activities. Near a mature expanse of grass there were picnic tables already occupied by families. There were blankets and chairs arranged nearby for folks who got there too late.

Park barbecues were smoking as town officials and volunteer chamber-of-commerce members were cooking hamburgers and hot dogs paid for out of community funds. He saw Tom McKnight and Mayor Goodson working together and brushing up against each other intimately, the way couples do.

Speaking of couples…

Burke took Syd's hand into his own. He sensed more than felt her want to pull away, but she didn't and he liked the feel of her fingers in his palm. Taking their relationship public was working for him in a big way.

"Lights, camera, action," he said.

They made their way along the path and greeted people. Burke was surprised how many he knew and Syd said hello to everyone. She stopped to chat with an older couple about their aging truck and he glanced up ahead. Violet Stewart, hostess at the diner and Syd's former friend, was there with two kids and a nice-looking man who was probably her husband…and the guy who had dumped Syd years ago. Burke knew when she spotted them because he felt her tense.

He leaned down to whisper in her ear. "We can take a detour."

"Not my style."

So they kept going and stopped by the young family. Burke nodded. "Hi, Vi."

"Burke." There was forced cheerfulness in the woman's voice. Her gaze drifted to Syd. "Hi."

"Hey." She looked at the man and it wasn't hard to tell this was the first time she'd seen him since all the bad stuff went down. "Charlie."

"How are you, Syd?"

"Good." She squeezed Burke's hand, then let it go. "Charlie Stewart, this is Burke Holden."

The two men shook hands and said all the right things while tension flowed like a swollen river between the two women.

"Well…we have to go meet my dad." Syd angled her head in the general direction of the barbecues.

"Yeah." There was a lot of regret in Violet's voice. "It was good to see you. Have fun, you two."

"Right. You guys, too. Later." Syd lifted a hand, then headed for the table near where her father was cooking.

Side by side they sat on the bench. Their shoulders brushed and heat that had nothing to do with the Montana sun shining above shot through him. Burke did his best to ignore the sensation because of the tricky situation.

Still, he was curious about something and they were far enough away from everyone not to be overheard. "How was it seeing Charlie again?" he asked.

"Weird," she said, glancing around at the people nearby watching her and the couple who had hurt her in the past.

"Weird bad or good?"

"Not bad," she admitted. "It's been a long time. I don't feel anything for him. But Violet—"

"She seems nice," he said.

"And how do you know?"

"I've seen her a lot in the diner. It's what happens when a guy—"

"Has to eat out in restaurants," she finished for him with a grin. It faded quickly. And there was wistfulness in her voice when she said, "She is nice. And they look good together. Two beautiful kids. A boy and girl. The perfect family."

"There's no such thing as perfect."

"I know. And that wasn't a bitter comment. Far from it." She met his gaze. "I envy her. I'm envious of them."

"So you want a family?"

She shrugged. "It's what my dad wants for me."

"What are you after?" he asked, really curious.

"It's easier to tell you what I *don't* want." She glanced around and people looked away. "This is the downside of small-town life. Call me stubborn, but I'm not going to give them anything to talk about. I intend to talk to Violet, but not when it would be a public spectacle."

"Good for you." He slung his arm across her shoulders and pulled her into a side hug, aware that she'd veered away from a thumb up or down on the topic of children and family. "Gossip may be a negative aspect of small-town life, but it works for our purposes. We're all about making a public spectacle of ourselves."

At that moment Tom McKnight turned to smile and wave at his daughter. She leaned in to Burke and put her hand on his jeans-covered thigh. Yeah, this arrangement was working for him in unexpectedly awesome ways.

When the coast was clear, she put some distance between them and removed her hand, curling her fingers into her palm as if it was scorched. Count him in on that.

"So," she said, clearing her throat. "You certainly have lots of acquaintances in town."

"There's a good reason for that."

"What might it be?" she asked sweetly.

"I'm dating the sweetheart of Blackwater Lake and everyone has gone out of their way to make my acquaintance. They're watching over you. The only hitch in the plan is that when we break up, they'll want to cut my heart out with a spoon."

"Only if you elope with my best friend."

"And who would that be?"

"I don't have one anymore." Her gaze was wistful when it shifted to the young family not far away. "But in the plus column we can consider this date number two."

"How do you figure? By my count this is our first."

"Don't forget dinner with Dad and Loretta."

"Ah." He didn't want to count that one because it was a double date and they hadn't been alone. Mostly it annoyed him to be counting down the times he would see her.

The depth of his reluctance to put a finite number of meetings on their arrangement was surprising. More and more he was realizing that she was the most intriguing woman he'd met in a very long time.

"How pathetic did you have to look to get Cam to invite you to dinner?" Syd asked Burke.

"No more than usual." He glanced over at her and grinned.

The day after the park dedication she was in the car beside him again. This was getting to be a habit and it was unclear as yet if that was a good thing or not. On the good side, he looked awfully sexy behind the wheel of this expensive, sporty car. She debated whether or not to tell him when winter arrived, which could be a matter of weeks because Montana weather could be unpredictable, he was going to want a four-wheel-drive vehicle. Knowing how he loved this car, she decided to keep the comment to herself.

She was more curious about something else than what car he would choose to drive on icy roads. "How do you feel about having Sunday dinner with my family?"

"I'm looking forward to it," he said.

"So how did the invitation come about?"

"After I dropped you off at home yesterday and came back to the lodge, I ran into Cam. She invited me then."

"Her idea?" Syd asked, teasing. She'd been with him in the bar when her sister-in-law talked to him about setting a date to meet her husband and daughter. "You didn't plead for a home-cooked meal?"

"I would have if I'd thought of it. But the word on the street is spreading about us and it was high time I met the rest of the McKnights."

"Okay, then."

Syd listened for even a tiny trace of nerves in his voice but heard nothing. Ice water in his veins, she thought. Probably for the best since she was nervous enough for both of them.

"You do know my brothers will be there, right? With their wives? And children. Small ones. Babies, really. Just adorably toddling around."

"You left out your dad and Loretta."

"They're not the ones I'm concerned about since we already had dinner with them. It's Alex and Ben. My brothers are no one's fools."

"You think they'll suspect we're trying to pull a fast one?"

"Dad is wary and he's probably said something to them."

"Then we'll have to lay it on thick." Something in his voice said he wouldn't mind that a bit.

Syd couldn't help the small ripple of pleasure at the thought. If she was being honest, getting cozy with him was a very appealing option.

Burke confidently and competently drove the car around the lake. From here it wasn't far to her brother's house. "This is a really beautiful area."

"I love it." The words were simple but incredibly heartfelt. "I can't imagine living anywhere else."

She looked at the water, where late-afternoon sun turned it a brilliant blue. Closer to the shoreline, shadows from the mountains and trees crept slowly toward the middle of the lake. "My brother Alex builds custom homes around here. He built Ben and Cam's and his own. Ellie, his wife, is an architect and drew up the plans."

"I'll have to talk to him about that."

"What? Are you thinking of moving here?" That surprised her for a lot of reasons.

"When the resort is booming, this area is going to be exclusive. Location, location. A second home would be a good investment."

For a moment she'd thought it might be personal, but not so much. He was a businessman, after all, and they had an agreement. There was nothing personal about that. Right now all she could worry about was getting through this family dinner unscathed.

Burke made a right turn into the driveway of Ben and Cam's home. He pulled to a stop beside her father's truck. Alex's car was there, too, which meant they were the last to arrive. Syd looked at the house and the bright lights coming from inside. There was a three-car garage and the front yard had an expanse of velvety green grass encircled by manicured bushes and flowers. They got out of the car and walked to the imposing double-door entry, where she pushed the doorbell.

"Here goes nothing," she muttered before the door was opened.

Camille Halliday McKnight stood there with her warm

welcoming smile. "Hi, you two. Glad you could join us, Burke. Come in."

"I'm grateful for the invitation. For a nomad like me restaurant food can get old."

"Syd…" Her sister-in-law's voice had a chiding note in it. "Shame on you for not having him over to dinner at your house."

They hadn't even been here a minute and she was busted already. If they were really dating she would have cooked for him. Cam's remark caught her completely off guard and she couldn't think of anything to say.

"She's mentioned it." Burke to the rescue with a loose interpretation of their understanding. "But I've been busy and we've been taking things slow. Didn't want to go public with this too soon."

"Like father, like daughter," Cam said, closing the door behind them. "I was completely surprised to find out your dad and the mayor had been secretly dating for a while."

"Go figure," Syd said. "We McKnights are an unconventional bunch."

"Come and meet everyone," Cam invited.

She led them through the large, two-story entry with an overhead chandelier, then into the spacious family room with connecting kitchen. Loretta was setting the table and Alex's wife was stirring something on the stove.

She waved and said, "I'm Ellie. Nice to meet you, Burke."

"Likewise," he said.

Her eighteen-month-old daughter, Leah, was sitting on the family room floor with her nearly two-year-old cousin, Amanda. The two little girls were surrounded by toys.

Alex and Ben stood with their father by the river-rock fireplace and all three turned to look at Sydney and Burke. She knew it wasn't possible but felt as if *fraud* was tattooed across her forehead. *Never let them see you sweat,* she thought, then slid her hand into Burke's and plastered a big smile on her face as they joined the group.

"Alex, Ben, this is Burke Holden." She watched as her brothers shook his hand, polite but suspicious.

"So you're going out with my baby sister," Alex said. He hadn't lost the oldest-brother protective streak he'd honed as the oldest boy looking out for his younger siblings.

"Yes." This time Burke didn't say "that's the rumor" because they really had gone out.

Syd knew her brother badly wanted to ask what his intentions were, but to his credit he held back.

Ben held out his hand. "I hear you're building a big resort."

"It's going to be a very successful endeavor for my company, but for Blackwater Lake, too. I was just saying to Syd that property values are going to go through the roof." He looked at Alex. "Your development here on the lake is going to be the place to live."

"We just hope it doesn't grow so fast that ancillary services can't keep up," Ben said. "Medical care for example."

"I've talked to the mayor about that and a hospital is going to be in the short-term plans. A small regional airport is going in simultaneously with the building near the ski resort."

"You've thought of everything," her dad said.

"Probably not, but the team and I are doing our best on this project. We don't want to mess it up."

"And we'd prefer that you don't," Alex said. "This is our home."

Syd listened and could read between the lines of what was being said. Watching their faces, she tried to see them objectively. Her brothers were about the same height as their father, a little over six feet, and both had brown eyes. Alex's hair was dark, almost black, while Ben's had highlights from the sun making it lighter. That was ironic since he was a doctor—an orthopedic specialist—and spent most of his time indoors. As a building contractor, Alex was outside most of the time.

"How do you like Blackwater Lake?" he asked.

"It's what I would call idyllic," Burke answered. "My cousin and partner, Sloan, is the one who brought the area to my attention a few years ago and we both agree on the potential."

Just then Syd felt a small hand on her leg and looked down to see blonde, blue-eyed Amanda smiling up at her. She babbled something that sounded a lot like "auntie."

"Hi, baby girl." Syd bent and picked up the toddler. "You're getting so big and even more beautiful than last week when I saw you."

Cam, sporting oven mitts, was looking on from the kitchen.

"You're just prejudiced, Auntie Syd."

"Definitely. And proud of it." She looked down when another little hand patted her leg. With dark hair and eyes, Leah favored her daddy, Alex. "Hi, munchkin. You're so big, too. And even more beautiful than when I saw you last week." She looked at Ellie, the child's mother, and said, "Gotta keep it even."

"Good for you, Auntie Syd." Ellie smiled fondly.

It was obvious the toddler wanted to be held, too, but Syd had her hands full. "I can't pick you up, sweetie."

As if Leah understood, she turned and slapped the closest leg, which happened to be Burke's. When your world perspective came from such a low center of gravity, probably all males in jeans looked like your daddy.

This could go one of two ways. Either the little one would get loud in her demands, or lose interest and move on. Neither of those things happened. It never occurred to Syd that Burke would voluntarily pick up Leah, but pick her up he did.

"Hey, little bit. How's life treating you?"

The little girl's smile showed off the fact that she was intrigued by the handsome stranger as so many women often were.

"I'll take her," Alex offered.

"That's okay." Burke studied the child in his strong arms. "She's a cutie. In about fifteen years both of your dads are going to have their hands full."

"Don't remind us." The look on Ben's face said he was rejecting that idea with every fiber of his being. "Dad's been doing a good job of rubbing that in since Amanda and Leah were born."

"I've been offering to pay for my granddaughters' room and board until age thirty-five at that convent in the Himalayas." Tom grinned at his sons. "God knows I wish I'd done that for your sister."

"You know I'm standing here, right?" Syd said.

"I do. And this isn't anything I haven't said to your face," her father replied.

"Okay, then." She snuggled the little girl in her arms more securely and kissed the chubby cheek. "Men can be so annoying."

"You know we're all standing here, right?" Burke said, one eyebrow lifted.

"Yes, but in case anyone missed it, I'd be happy to say it louder," she offered.

"We got the message." Alex seemed unfazed. "And just so you know, there's not a zinger you can come up with that would keep me from protecting my little girl as long as I live. Or any other important woman in my life for that matter." He slid an unmistakably protective look at her and Burke seemed to get the message.

"Well said." Burke nodded slightly, letting the other man know he understood.

The little girl he was holding patted his cheek to get

his attention, then pointed to the pile of toys in the center of the room. At the same time, Amanda was squirming to get down, so Syd complied and set her on the rug, where she looked up then at the playthings and grunted.

"Offhand I'd say we're being drafted for duty," Burke commented.

"I wasn't sure you were picking up the signals." She shrugged. "You don't have to. I can handle this."

When he put Leah down, she grabbed his hand and leaned her tiny body in the direction she wanted to go. His smile was full of boyish charm guaranteed to melt female hearts from coast to coast and Syd was no exception.

"This little girl is not going to take no for an answer," he said. "Let's do this."

"Okay," Syd said to Cam, Ellie and Loretta, who were busy with dinner prep. "We would help you guys in the kitchen but these girls are determined to play."

"Trust me," Ben said behind her. "If you play with them, that is helping in the kitchen."

"Good. Works for me."

She and Burke sat on the beige rug near the toys and let the toddlers hand them dolls, plastic cell phones and a scaled-down pink play stroller. Her nieces were chattering in a language no one could understand with the possible exception of their moms. She watched Burke, trying to decide if he was really this good-natured or just a gifted actor who would really rather take a sharp stick in the eye than play with girl toys.

The thing was, she didn't think he was that talented a performer and got the feeling he really liked kids. This high-powered, focused, *über*successful CEO was a sucker for children.

Color her surprised.

About fifteen minutes later Cam and Ellie directed their husbands to take the babies upstairs for a diaper change, adding that dinner would be ready in about thirty minutes. The dads grabbed up their daughters and disappeared as ordered. Syd enjoyed seeing her big strong brothers tamed. It was a sign that they were happy to be settled down with two exceptional women who loved them.

Still in troop-commander mode, Cam told Syd that she should give Burke a tour of the backyard. A look in her sister-in-law's eyes said she was being given a break and should take advantage.

Syd nodded then said to Burke, "Want to see the backyard?"

"Sure."

Her dad grinned at Loretta. "Since diaper duty has already been assigned, I'll help you with whatever you're doing."

The mayor smiled back. "That means looking over my shoulder and critiquing."

"Maybe." The twinkle in Tom McKnight's eyes was good to see.

Syd wondered why she hadn't noticed that before her father's secret relationship had been outed. For better or worse, now that she had noticed, she would do everything in her power to keep that happy look right where it was.

Burke stood and held out his hand to help her up. When she was on her feet, he didn't let go. Between the warm, cozy feeling of her fingers in his and the adorable image of him playing with the girls, Sydney wasn't so sure it was a good idea to be alone with him. But it wasn't about her or what she wanted, so she led him to the French doors that would take them outside.

Strategically placed lights illuminated the brick patio and outside furniture. There was a pool and spa in the center of the yard and a gazebo in the far corner that overlooked the lake below in the distance. Like the front, there was an abundance of grass and shrubs. This place was like something out of a fairy tale, Syd thought.

"This is Ben's backyard," she announced.

"I would never have guessed." Burke looked around. "It's beautifully done."

"I couldn't agree more." She removed her hand from his and folded her arms over her chest. "So, we got over that hurdle. First meeting of the whole family."

"They all seem very nice."

"Even though my brother Alex subtly threatened you?" she asked.

"I respect his instinct to look after the people he cares about."

"You know he really won't beat you up when our quote-unquote romance goes south, right?"

"If he decided to, I think I could hold my own. I actually envy him," Burke said. "Both of your brothers."

"Why?"

"They've got it all. The things money can't buy, I mean."

In the lengthening shadows of dusk it was difficult to read the emotion on his face, but she got the distinct impression that there was regret in his voice. It occurred to her that she didn't know a lot about him. She hadn't asked too many questions, feeling that it wasn't right to pry, what with him doing her such a huge favor. But now she was curious.

He hadn't responded when she'd wondered out loud if his son's mother would object to Liam spending time here in Blackwater Lake. So all she really knew was that he was amicably divorced and the custody agreement had been harmonious as well. He'd asked about her past and she'd said you show me yours and I'll show you mine. But he'd only agreed that she would need to know as it pertained to their agreement.

Now, for some reason, she needed to know. "So, I have some questions."

Chapter Six

"You mentioned your cousin. Are you an only child?" Syd asked.

"Yes. Sloan is like the brother I never had. We're pretty close."

"And you have a son." Syd felt like an attorney interrogating a witness, but the questions kept popping into her mind.

"He's the best thing I ever did." But again there was regret in his voice.

"Tell me about his mother," she said.

"What do you want to know?"

"Good question." She shrugged. "Do you get along? Is she a good mom?"

"No."

There wasn't a shred of doubt in his tone. "But you said the divorce and custody negotiations were amicable."

"Because when I asked for sole custody she didn't argue. She didn't want him. She'd lost both of her parents

a while ago and the echo of divorce and custody negotiations had barely died away when she moved to Paris."

"But she's been back to see her son."

"No."

Sydney was shocked speechless. You heard about this
sort of thing in news stories, movies and books, but she'd
never known of anyone in real life experiencing it.

When she could speak, she asked, "Who looks out for
him?"

"The housekeeper. She's been with me since before he
was born. I tease about getting custody of her in the divorce." He smiled. "She loves Liam like her own."

"So there was no one to object if you'd brought Liam
to Blackwater Lake for the summer."

"No. But all his friends are there in Chicago. His activities. His schedule and routine. I finally decided that
stability for him was the most important thing."

"More than having his dad?" She frowned, puzzled.
"The details could be worked out and it would be an adjustment for him, but I would think that having him close
by would be good for you both. You could take an afternoon off. Have lunch together. Work at home when he's
asleep. Where there's a will…"

Frowning, he looked down at her. "You feel strongly
about this."

She nodded. "My dad was a single father and ran a business. He raised my brothers and me. Granted, Blackwater
Lake is a place where folks pitch in to help their own, but
Dad was there at night. To read me bedtime stories and
tuck me in. He checked out my homework and my boy-
friends. He was *there*."

"You don't hold back, do you?"

"There's very little point in that." She shrugged. "I call
'em as I see 'em."

"I can't decide if you're being supportive or trying to make me feel guilty."

"I get the feeling that you don't need any help with a guilt complex, Burke."

"You're right. I decided a long time ago that feeling responsible for the bad stuff is a natural by-product of being a divorced father. That's how I make peace with it."

"I can't believe his mother didn't want him."

He shook his head. "To her he was a mistake and she always treated him that way. It's a sad reality that as bad a father as I am, I'm better than his mother."

"I just can't wrap my mind around doing something like that," she said.

"Because you obviously like children. You're good with them."

"I just give them whatever they want." She laughed. "It's what an aunt does."

"Clearly those little girls adore you."

"Because I never say no unless it's something that will hurt them."

"I remember those days with Liam." His voice was filled with wistfulness and regret. "It was simpler then."

There was such sadness and self-reproach in the words that she felt an overwhelming urge to put her arms around him, comfort him. The next best thing was to change the mood. "Tell me about him," she suggested.

"He's bright and funny. Athletic. Just a great kid. I really hate the feeling that I'm screwing him up. You only get one shot with a kid."

Something about that statement sounded final, as if he'd already blown any chance to get it right. Intellectually she understood that everyone's approach to parenting each child was unique, but she had a feeling that's not what he meant.

He'd said he envied her brothers, their families. He'd commented that Sloan was like a brother to him, implying that he'd wanted siblings. Because of that Syd would have thought he wouldn't want his son to be an only child.

"It won't always be just the two of you, Burke. Surely when you meet the right person you'll want to add to your family."

He shook his head. "No."

"But why?"

"I found out I'm not good at marriage, for one thing. And more important, I wouldn't want another child to have me for a father."

At that moment the French door behind them opened and Cam's voice drifted out. "Dinner's ready."

"We'll be right there," Syd answered automatically. When the door closed again, she said, "Burke, I think you're being too hard on yourself—"

"You're wrong. Let's go inside and eat." Clearly he didn't want to talk about this anymore.

Syd had suddenly lost her appetite. He was so good with kids and really seemed to enjoy them. It was hard to believe he was as bad at parenting as he so obviously believed.

But why should she care what he believed? Why should it matter so much?

What they had was a relationship of convenience. They both had their reasons for putting on this act. It had all made sense until she'd seen him holding that little girl in his arms and the gentle way he'd played with both of her nieces.

There would never be anything serious between her and Burke Holden. But that didn't stop her from feeling as if his revelation had cost her something really important.

Something that mattered very much.

* * *

A week later, first thing Monday morning Sydney grabbed a cup of coffee and a donut from the customer waiting area at McKnight Auto, then headed for the exit that went outside to the service bay. Her father's office was on the way and she stopped in the doorway. From this position she could see out the window in case someone drove up. From out of nowhere Burke's image popped into her mind.

He'd come by twice and both were memorable. The first time she'd asked him to participate in a crazy scheme to convince her father she had a boyfriend. The second time he'd kissed her, the kind of kiss that made her want to put up a commemorative plaque that said, Burke Holden Kissed Me Beside the Hydraulic Lift.

Earth to Syd, she thought. Focus.

"Morning, Dad."

He looked up from his computer. "Hi, Syd."

She took a bite of donut and the white powdered sugar sprinkled the front of her work shirt. It was probably the most benign substance that would muck up her clothes today, but getting dirty didn't bother her. From the time she was a little girl, she'd always liked it. Oil and transmission fluid were the lifeblood of a car and part of the tools of her trade. The purr of a repaired engine was music to her ears.

And the man sitting behind the desk was the one who'd taught her everything she knew. She liked to touch base with him in the morning before they both got busy. They lived under the same roof, but somehow this quiet time before the day started was when important things were shared. And the man had spent most of his time at Loretta's house lately so there wasn't much time to chat. In the days since the family dinner at Cam and Ben's she hadn't seen much of her dad except at work.

"You and Burke do anything over the weekend?" he asked.

"No." Syd had no intention of asking him what he and the mayor had been doing.

"What's wrong with him?" her father demanded.

"I'm not sure what you mean."

"Your brothers tell me they liked him. He seems an upstanding sort."

That's the way she pegged Burke, too. "Alex and Ben are pretty smart."

For once, fate had dropped a good man in her lap. He was handsome, funny and seemed to get along well with the adult males in her family as well as being great with kids. Dinner had been really fun. He fit in and for once she hadn't been the odd one out. She'd had a date, albeit a fake one. It was nice not being alone. Which made her sad when she thought about what he'd told her in the backyard.

"I say again—what's wrong with him? Letting a pretty girl like you be alone on Friday and Saturday. If he doesn't step up, some other fella is going to come along and squeeze him out."

She felt a stab of guilt for the deception and was *this* close to coming clean. But her dad looked so happy and lighthearted. In her whole life she'd never seen his eyes twinkle like this and the spring in his step made him seem ten years younger. She didn't want anything to change that. Still, she could use this opportunity to nudge him where she thought he should go.

"You should listen to yourself and take your own advice." She finished her donut.

Tom stood and walked around the desk. "What does that mean?"

"If you don't seal the deal and marry Loretta pretty soon, some other fella will steal her right out from under your nose. She won't wait forever."

"Maybe I'll seal the deal." His eyebrows drew together. "Or maybe not."

She was about to call him out on that but a minivan pulled up outside. "Got a customer."

Her father turned to look as a woman exited the vehicle. "Uh-oh. That's Violet Walker—"

"It's Stewart now," Syd reminded him.

"I can write up the work order. I understand if you don't want to."

He told her that he hadn't mentioned Violet being back in town because of not wanting to remind her of that painful time. He'd hoped she and Violet wouldn't run into each other. And that had worked out so well, she'd wanted to say. No, she had to deal with this. It was an opportunity and she realized she'd been waiting for one.

"It's okay." She met her father's gaze. "Took a lot of guts for her to come here. I want to talk to her."

"That's my girl. I'll be right here if you need me." He dropped a kiss on the top of her head and went back to his computer work.

Syd dropped her disposable coffee cup in the trash by the door then grabbed a clipboard with service form already attached. She walked outside and met her former BFF face-to-face beneath the overhang connecting the office to the service bay.

"Hi, Violet."

"Sydney." She looked tense but determined. "The van needs an oil change. I would take it somewhere else, but this is the only place in town. I hope it's okay, but if not—"

"Of course it's okay."

"Charlie offered to bring it in, but I said it would be better this way."

"That would have been fine. But, the fact is, I've been wanting to talk to you ever since that day at the park."

"Really?" There was eagerness in the single word before a wary expression tightened her features. "Why?"

"To clear the air." She smiled. "It's a small town."

"Yeah. That's one of the reasons Charlie and I moved back. For our parents, but also because this is a great place to raise kids."

"And we're going to run into each other."

Vi nodded. "I could feel everyone at the park watching to see what would happen between us."

"Me, too. I'd have said something to you then, but it was more fun to give the people of Blackwater Lake *nothing* to talk about."

"I know what you mean." A small smile eased some of the tension. "It always bugged you when people gossiped."

"Because we couldn't get away with anything." A series of long-ago memories scrolled through Syd's mind like a video. "If I spit on the sidewalk, someone would tell my dad."

"I know." Violet grinned. "Remember that time we decided to run away and join the circus?"

"Oh, gosh—" Syd laughed and nodded. "I haven't thought about that for years. We cut school and went to the grocery store to buy snacks with our allowances. Thinking ahead for the road trip."

"Not far enough ahead." Vi chuckled at the memory. "I'm not quite sure what we were going to be in the circus or why we thought they would hire us even if we happened to run across one."

"Fortunately it didn't get that far because someone called my dad."

"And my parents," she added. "To this day I have no idea who ratted us out."

"I have my suspicion although it was never confirmed. It's my theory that there's some kind of parental code of silence," Syd said. "And you're one of them. Look at you.

A mom now and Charlie's a dad. Two beautiful kids—a boy and girl."

"Right? Todd and Bailey are the best things Charlie and I ever did."

Syd knew for a fact that she didn't begrudge this woman her life or have any animosity about the past. But envy was something else. Violet was once her best friend and now she had a husband, children. She had everything Syd wanted. It was everything Syd's dad wanted for her so that he could move forward with his own life.

But the everything she wanted had always been vague until recently, Syd realized. Somehow Burke had made it come into focus.

"You and Charlie have a beautiful family, Vi," she said softly.

"Syd, I'm sorry. We never meant for it to happen and you have to know that neither of us would deliberately hurt you. You're our friend. At least you were," Violet added.

"I know." Clearly Violet had heard the wistfulness in Syd's voice but it had nothing to do with what happened all those years ago. She reached out and touched the other woman's arm, squeezing reassuringly. "It's obvious that he didn't love me or he wouldn't have fallen so hard for you."

"You have to know I didn't do anything. I never came on to him and he didn't to me, either. It's just that we all hung out together. Charlie and I felt the attraction. We both tried to fight the feelings but couldn't. We should have talked to you but eloping seemed like a good idea at the time. I just feel awful about what happened and the way we handled it. And so does Charlie."

"What do you say we put it behind us?"

"Are you sure?" There was hope in the other woman's eyes. "I think that would be wonderful, but can you forgive and forget?"

"No doubt about it. I already have."

"That's really a load off my mind." Violet's smile was genuine and relaxed now. "I'm so glad."

"Me, too." She studied her friend—maybe not best friends forever, but definitely friends again. "And I have to say that you look fantastic. You were always beautiful, but the whole maternal, wifely thing is working for you. What's your secret? You're positively glowing."

"Funny you should phrase it like that." She paused dramatically. "I'm going to have another baby."

"Oh, my. Congratulations." Syd honestly meant it, even though that pesky envy poked her again. "That's wonderful. Is Charlie happy about it?"

"Ecstatic."

Lucky Violet, she thought.

Every life was filled with peaks and valleys, but this news seemed to make her own valley even deeper. It was off the map of reason, but when Burke had said unequivocally that his future did not have a place in it for more children, Syd had been disappointed on a level that made no sense.

Now the news of her friend's pregnancy made her disappointment even more acute.

There was an explanation for this reaction, but she didn't even want to think about it. She took his revelation as a warning to avoid trouble ahead. If the incident with Violet and Charlie had taught her anything it was that knowing the bad was better than getting blindsided.

After work Sydney walked into Bar None, Blackwater Lake's local drinking establishment. It was rugged and rustic, with dark beams overhead and a wood plank floor. Illumination came from lantern-shaped lights scattered throughout the place in booths and on tables. In the center of the room was the big, rectangular oak bar with brass foot rail. This was a weeknight so not many of the swivel stools were occupied, but a quick glance at the men and women told her none of them were the friend she was meeting.

She scanned the booths lining the exterior then spotted a woman waving. Maggie Potter was sitting at a bistro table in the far corner and Syd headed that way.

She hoisted herself up onto the chair across from her friend. "Hi."

"Hey, yourself." The pretty, dark-eyed brunette smiled.

"Sorry I'm late. Have you been here long?"

"Just a few minutes. Long enough to order our usual."

White wine. This was a standing date for them and nine times out of ten a glass of Chardonnay was involved along with something to eat. The food was different from the diner, which was a more family-oriented place. Bar None had a happy-hour menu that suited Syd and Maggie, two single ladies on the town.

"So, where's that adorable little girl of yours tonight?"

A tender expression settled on Maggie's face. "She's staying with Uncle Brady and her soon-to-be-official Aunt Olivia. Just between you and me, I think they want to start a family soon and are practicing on Danielle."

"Have they set a date?"

"No. All we get are a lot of maybe Christmas. Or Valentine's Day. I think it will be spur-of-the-moment. And small."

"Sounds nice."

Maggie nodded. "In the meantime I'm happy to let them dote on my little girl. I love Danielle more than anything, but I do so enjoy a break from her."

Syd figured that was because her friend was both mother and father to the child. Maggie's husband had been a soldier and died in Afghanistan before his daughter was born.

She thought about Burke, a single father who thought

he was doing a bad job of parenting. She didn't believe that. The reality was that sometimes kids got dealt a lousy hand but that didn't mean they couldn't thrive in spite of it.

Just then the owner of the establishment carried over two glasses of wine. Delanie Carlson was somewhere in her twenties, a curvy, blue-eyed redhead. She'd inherited Bar None when her father passed away last year. Syd knew that she'd gone through some rough times financially and was one of the Blackwater Lake business owners who would benefit from the resort being built. To make ends meet, she'd rented out rooms over the bar, but there was bound to be a spike in revenue during construction as well as when the visitor count jumped after opening.

"Here you go, ladies." Delanie put a wineglass in front of each of them. "Are you ready to order or do you need another minute?"

Syd glanced at her unopened menu. "I haven't had a chance to look over the choices."

Dee grinned. "It hasn't changed since last week. Or the week before that. Or—"

"Are you implying I should know it by heart?"

"*Implying* would be more diplomatic than saying straight out that surely you have it memorized by now. So I guess you could say I'm just implying."

Syd laughed. "It's a good thing we're friends or I could take that the wrong way."

"Okay. Enjoy the wine. I'll be back."

Maggie watched the bar owner walk away, then said, "Speaking of friends...I heard you and Violet ran into each other at the park dedication. How did that go?"

"If it hadn't been civilized, you wouldn't have to ask." She took a sip of her wine and savored the crisp, cold liquid. "Coincidentally, I saw her today at the shop. She brought her car in for service."

Maggie's dark eyes widened. "Wow. Is there anything I should know?"

"We talked. She apologized, which wasn't necessary since she already did a long time ago. I just wasn't ready to listen then." She shrugged. "They're happy and have a beautiful family."

"And you're envious," her friend commented.

"Not that she's with Charlie. Just that she has a husband and children." Syd remembered the news. "And she's pregnant again. I'm happy for her. And I'm so over what happened."

"So you're friends again?"

"I'd say so. Not like we were but—" Syd was distracted when the front door opened and Burke walked in. He glanced around as if looking for someone, then his gaze settled on her and he headed over.

"What a pleasant surprise. You didn't mention you'd be here tonight." He leaned in and gave her a quick kiss.

"I didn't?"

She knew she hadn't because the information was on a need-to-know basis and he didn't need to know. He was playing the part of boyfriend to perfection and she couldn't help wondering why he was so good at deception. She needed to act like his girlfriend and found it far too easy to do that. And, gosh darn it, she wanted a much longer kiss than that paltry peck on the mouth. She felt as if her head was going to explode.

"I don't think we've met. Burke Holden," he said to Maggie.

She shook his hand. "Maggie Potter. I own the ice cream parlor and the adjacent lunch counter with my business partner. I've heard you've been in and I'm sorry I missed you. I'm always in the office upstairs."

Syd resisted the urge to shake her head to clear it.

"Maggie and I get together here at Bar None about once a week for a girls' night."

"I didn't mean to interrupt."

"That's okay," Maggie said. "It's nice to finally put a name and face together."

And what a face he had, Syd wanted to say. If only he was shallow the way so many handsome men were, their understanding would be much less complicated.

"It's nice to meet you, Maggie." He looked at the door when it opened and a man walked in. "Speaking of meeting…I'm here on business and he just walked in."

"Don't let us keep you." Syd made the mistake of looking into his deep blue eyes and felt as if she'd been sucked into a vortex. The problem was that she didn't know whether or not she wanted out.

"I wish you *could* keep me," he said with feeling. "It would be a lot more fun. Even if I did crash a girls' night." There was genuine regret in the look he gave Maggie. "I hope I'll see you again soon."

"Me, too."

"I'll call you, Syd." And then he walked over and shook hands with the newcomer before settling in a booth on the other side of the bar.

She might not be able to see him, but Syd knew he was in the room. All his intensity just seemed to alter the molecular composition of air.

"So," Maggie said. "Is he the reason you're over Violet stealing your boyfriend?"

"I was over it long before Burke came to town."

"Okay," her friend said. "Looked to me as if you like him a lot."

"Really?" Syd met her friend's gaze. "What did I do?"

"Hard to put into words. Just a feeling." Maggie looked thoughtful. "The best way to describe it is that you looked at Burke the way Olivia does my brother, Brady. And she's in love with him."

Oh, dear God. It didn't mean anything. Really, it was all about reacting to a good-looking man and had nothing to do with deeper feelings, she told herself.

She just hoped herself wasn't telling a lie.

"We're just good friends," she explained.

"I hope so." There was concern swirling in Maggie's eyes. "Because I've heard he's here to get the resort project going."

"I'm not sure why that bothers you but I can see that it does."

"I'm worried because his home is in Chicago. Or so I've been told."

"That's true," Sydney confirmed.

"Have you thought about what happens to you when he leaves Blackwater Lake to go back to his home base? I don't think it's a stretch to say that you're not open to relocating."

True, Syd thought. Her family was here and so was her job. But it was more than that. Someday she would take over the business her father had built.

"We've talked a little." That wasn't a complete lie. They did talk when together. Just not about where they were going from here because there was no *here.* "We just figure that things will work out when the time comes."

That also wasn't a lie. In the beginning they'd talked about what would happen at the end. So, she was beginning to get the hang of telling half truths. Her father would be so proud.

"Please don't think I'm prying. I just don't want to see you hurt again," Maggie said.

"I understand." And she did. But enough about her. "So how's the business expansion working for you?"

"Good." Maggie sipped her wine. "I'm planning to run

an ad in the paper to rent out my two upstairs bedrooms to pay for it."

Syd picked up her wineglass and took a sip, then asked, "Why?"

"I have a business loan and need to put away all the money I can. Just in case."

"But your brother owns a very successful technology company. Call it a wild guess, but wouldn't he help you out if necessary?"

"Yes. But I wouldn't ask or take anything from him." Her friend's dark eyes grew darker, a sign she was thinking about the husband she'd lost far too soon. "It's something I need to do on my own. For Danny. When we got married it was clear that my brother was on his way and would be incredibly successful. Danny was always trying to prove himself. He wouldn't have wanted me to take Brady's help."

"And renting the rooms?"

"Everyone knows when construction starts on the resort there will be a shortage of places to live. I already have someone lined up, an older woman I know who lost her husband, too. And anyone else who expresses interest in the other room for rent can be checked out. I've already talked to Sheriff Fletcher about that." She shrugged. "There's an outside entrance, which makes the upstairs more separate. I'll provide breakfast and dinner. It's all worked out. It's very trendy and can be really lucrative."

Syd recalled what Burke had said about the scarcity of places to stay here in Blackwater Lake. There was a lot of potential for profit. And when it came to the husband Maggie had lost, Syd had learned that there was no changing Maggie's mind once it was made up.

"I'm sure it will work out great," she said.

Just then Delanie came over and it was time to put in

their orders. While her friend chatted with the bar owner, Syd heard Burke's laugh from the other side of the room.

At some point she wouldn't have the opportunity to run in to him anywhere in Blackwater Lake because he would be gone. His leaving eventually was what made him perfect for this assignment. The fact that he lived somewhere else would be a convenient excuse for an amicable breakup. Before that happened, hopefully her father would feel comfortable enough about his daughter's future to marry Loretta. And when the time was right, Syd would end her charade with Burke.

The sooner the better—because far too often she looked at him and started thinking, what if they really had something? The problem was that *something* opened the door to everything and that was the foundation for pain and disappointment.

Wondering what might have been came with no risk and she was good with that.

Chapter Seven

Burke wasn't a spontaneous guy. So, by definition, buying a bouquet of flowers and heading to a woman's house without calling first to ask her to dinner was something he didn't do.

Except he was doing it.

He was almost to Sydney's house with flowers and planned to ask her to dinner. A fancy dinner at Fireside. It wasn't clear whether the high altitude and lack of oxygen here in the Montana mountains was causing this uncharacteristic behavior, or if there was something else going on. Whatever was responsible didn't matter. When the idea had popped into his mind, he couldn't shake it loose no matter how hard he tried. And he'd definitely tried.

He turned the car into her driveway and parked in front of the house. It was a modest-sized beige craftsman-style with a porch, two dormers and chocolate-brown shutters framing the windows. The two vehicles there belonged to Syd and her dad, which meant they were both home. So far, so good.

He grabbed the cellophane-wrapped bouquet resting on the passenger seat, hoping she hadn't started dinner yet. If so, he planned to charm her into putting it away for tomorrow. After exiting the car, he walked to the front door and rang the bell.

Almost immediately Tom McKnight answered, car keys in hand. Apparently he was on his way out. Looking at the flowers he said, "For me? You shouldn't have."

"If I'd known you were a bouquet kind of guy, I'd have brought two. But these are for Sydney."

"Nice move." Tom nodded approvingly. "I'm on my way to Loretta's and I think I'm going to take a play from your book. Where'd you get these?"

"The grocery store on Main Street. Although I'm told there won't be any soon. In the fall and winter it's a challenge to stock them."

"Thanks for the tip." Her father met his gaze. "Syd didn't say anything. Did she know you were coming?"

"No. I wanted to surprise her. Take her to dinner."

Again the man nodded his approval. "As the ladies would say, you're not just another pretty face, Holden. You've got style. But don't keep her out too late."

"Yes, sir."

"'Bye, Syd. Don't expect me back tonight. And Burke is here," he called over his shoulder before walking to his truck.

Moments later Syd stood in the doorway and was staring at the flowers as if they were an especially big, hairy spider. "What are you doing here?"

"I came to see you."

"With flowers?" Her tone said that was a breach of contract.

"Yes." He noted her skeptical expression. "Unless it's illegal in Montana for a guy to surprise a girl with flowers."

"It's definitely a surprise."

For him, too. This wasn't going quite the way he'd thought it would. "In case it's not clear, these are for you."

"Thanks." She took the bouquet he offered but held it as if she expected something to jump out and bite her.

"What's wrong?"

"That's what I'd like to know."

"Does there have to be a crisis for me to bring flowers and ask you to put on that little black dress so I can take you to dinner?"

"Yeah. Kind of. Our agreement isn't about bouquets and surprises—" She stopped and her eyes widened as if a light went on. "Oh, I get it. Nice move."

That's the second time a McKnight had said those words to him but he had a sneaking suspicion each of them meant something different.

"Can I come in?" he asked.

"Oh. Sure." She stepped back as he entered, then closed the door behind him.

"So," he said, "what is it you think I'm doing?"

"This 'surprise' is all about convincing Dad that we're a couple."

"Actually, I—"

"It's a great idea, Burke. And it worked better than you probably even expected."

"How so?" He certainly hadn't expected this but he wouldn't call it better.

"You surprise me with flowers and dinner in front of Dad. Color him impressed. But he's on his way to Loretta's and won't be back tonight." She beamed as if that's all there was to it.

"And?" he prompted.

"Dad bought the act completely. He thinks you walk on water and you don't even have to take me out."

Burke didn't know whether to shake her or kiss her. But since it appeared that she was trying to get out of spending time with him, he figured the best move was to do none of the above.

"What if I want to take you out?"

She blinked up at him as if that question came from out of nowhere. "Then I would have to say that comes under the heading of changing the rules. Seriously, I really appreciate your help. But I think we can consider this date number two." Apparently she noticed his frown because she added, "I'm just trying to make this as easy as possible for you."

That attitude in a woman was refreshing. His ex had always seemed to make things as hard as possible. Except with their son. She'd wanted no part of the responsibility of raising a child. In its own way, that was hard, too. Not for him, but for Liam.

"I'm not sure we should be counting dates," he finally said. "Things should unfold organically."

"That word. *Organic.* What does it mean? Why can't people just say natural?" The wary look was back. "We agreed to a certain number of times going out. Why shouldn't we count?"

"Because I really want to take you to dinner."

"Again I have to ask—why?"

That was the big question and he didn't have a really good answer. The truth was that ever since running in to her at Bar None last night, he couldn't stop thinking about her. He'd wanted to kiss her. Technically he had done that, but it wasn't the way he really wanted to kiss her. Since he couldn't get her off his mind, it followed that he wanted to see her tonight. If he had to put a finer point on this he'd chalk it up to loneliness, to living in a hotel without the comforts of home or family. That was as complicated as he was willing to get.

"I don't like eating alone." He slid his fingers into the pockets of his suit pants. "Look at it as doing me a favor."

"And I can't go like this?" She was weakening.

He inspected her yellow T-shirt, thin and worn in the most interesting places just like her jeans, and bare feet with hot-pink painted toenails. A need that had nothing to do with food tightened inside him. He would give almost anything to get her out of those clothes until all she had on was the sexy polish on her toes.

He cleared his throat. "As fetching as you look, your outfit is more appropriate for the diner than Fireside."

"Really? You want to spring for a nice dinner?"

"Yes." When she opened her mouth to protest, he put a finger to her lips to stop the words. "Don't ask me why."

"I wasn't going to."

"Yes, you were." He turned her toward the stairs. "Now go change. I'm starving."

"And I'm getting the most expensive meal on the menu," she said over her shoulder as she hurried up the stairs.

And worth every penny, he thought.

While waiting for her to change, he stared out the front window and savored his triumph. He was looking forward to spending the evening with a beautiful woman. There was something to be said for overcoming a challenge, but the truth was he wouldn't have taken no for an answer.

He hadn't had to work this hard for a date since he was a teenager, and probably not even then. For some reason he felt more satisfaction from wearing down Syd than he'd ever felt with any other woman.

Syd looked across the candlelit table at Burke. She was having a wonderful time since agreeing to come here. But flowers? A surprise dinner invitation from her pretend boyfriend? Who could blame her for being skittish? This…thing…between her and Burke Holden was feeling less like an agreement and more like *dating*.

At the moment she couldn't find the will to care what it was called. She'd made good on her vow to order the most expensive item on the menu. Actually Burke had asked if she liked steak and lobster. When she'd said yes, he told the waiter she would have that. It was too much food so she'd scarfed down the lobster and the steak was going to be tomorrow's lunch. Now she was rocking a lovely wine glow and sharing a piece of the best chocolate cake in Montana with the handsome man who'd brought her here.

And how cute was he?

A question she had no desire to answer because it opened the door to stuff she would rather not think about. Preferably ever.

"I'll be sure to let Uncle John know how nice you're being to me," she teased. "We could take a selfie and text it to him."

"No, we can't."

"Has anyone ever told you that you're a stick-in-the-mud?"

"I've been called worse," he said.

"Tell me."

He shook his head. "It's not something I'm comfortable repeating in polite company."

"Who said I was polite?" she responded.

"Maybe not, but you're a woman."

The way his voice dropped and got all husky on that word put a hitch in her breathing. His eyes took on an expression that was focused and intense, making her wonder what he would do if they were alone. And speaking of alone, she had a question.

"So you don't like eating by yourself?"

"I prefer company." The corner of his mouth curved up.

She dragged her fork through the thick chocolate icing, then looked at him. "Realistically you could have talked almost anyone in Blackwater Lake into going to dinner with you. But you brought me flowers and showed up without warning to surprise me. Why?"

"I'm particular about dinner companions. How would it look if I brought another woman here?" He met her gaze. "We haven't accomplished our mission yet."

"I guess, based on our original agreement, I just don't understand why you would go to so much trouble," she said.

"Okay, let me explain." He set down his fork and met her gaze. "I like you, Sydney. Sooner or later I would have asked you out if you hadn't hit on me first."

"I didn't hit on you," she protested. "You were just in the wrong place at the wrong time. If Phil the plumber had driven up at that moment I'd have hit on—" She stopped and cleared her throat. "I mean, I would have asked for his help with my problem."

"Maybe." His tone said he didn't believe that for a minute. "The fact is we did meet. And I agreed to your proposal. Although I don't think the ruse is necessary."

Aha, he had a purpose. The flowers and surprise were about sweetening the deal. "So you think I should tell my dad the truth? You want out of the agreement because you don't want to see me?"

"Not at all. I agreed to help move your father along in the courting process. Although I don't think the ruse is necessary to accomplish that objective."

"Why not?"

"Because your father will get where he needs to be when it feels right to him. And not because you are or are not in a committed relationship of your own."

"Then why are you helping me?" she asked.

"I very much want to see you. That's what the flowers and surprise were all about."

"You want to date me?"

"Yes."

On a scale of one to ten this was a fifteen on the surprise scale. "Why?"

His expression was ironic, as if to say "you really don't know?"

"Because I want to get to know you better. You're a beautiful and interesting woman."

"Wow." This was a first for her and she didn't know what to say to that.

"I like you. I'm attracted to you."

Translation: he wanted to sleep with her. She let that idea kick around for a few seconds and realized she had no opposition to that scenario.

"Okay."

"But I feel the necessity to be completely honest. I'm not the kind of guy your father wants for you."

"And you know this…how?"

"I meant what I said that night in your brother's backyard. I've been married and don't plan to do it again. There won't be more children. The only commitment I can make is to be Liam's father and do what's best for him."

"That's as it should be," she agreed.

"So, what do you say?"

"I don't remember the question," she lied.

"Are you okay with us going out? Having fun. No strings, no promises?"

She was much more comfortable with pretending to have fun with him, but had to admit she always had fun with him and that had nothing to do with their deal. That reaction was unexpected although maybe she should have expected something considering how strong her attraction had been to him from the beginning.

"Syd?"

She looked up. "Can I think about it?"

"Of course." He reached across the table and rested his hand over hers. "And whatever your answer is, I will keep my word in regard to our agreement."

"That's very decent of you."

"I'm a decent guy."

His sudden grin would melt the heart of any woman who was still breathing and Syd was no exception. How was she supposed to resist that?

The intensity was starting to close in on her. "You call yourself decent? In spite of the worst unrepeatable things people have said about you?"

"They were just frustrated."

He lifted a hand to signal the waiter for the check. When it was taken care of, they left the restaurant and walked outside to his car.

"It's a beautiful night." Syd took a deep breath, pulling the cool, clean mountain air into her lungs. "I love this time of year. Soaking up the good weather for as long as possible."

"Does the cold get to you? Chicago winters are pretty intense, too."

"No." She thought about the question. "I guess I'm used to subzero temperatures from time to time."

"You basically work outside," he pointed out.

"I'm used to that, too." She shrugged. "There are portable heaters for the service bay and ways to block out the most bitter cold. It helps that I love what I do."

"And you're good at it." He unlocked the car, opened the passenger door and guided her inside.

From the time she'd first expressed an interest in boys, her father had said she shouldn't go out with a guy who didn't open doors for a woman. He'd raised her brothers to do that and it seemed Burke had learned the lesson from someone. If she was doing a pro-and-con list to decide whether or not to take him up on his dating offer, being a gentleman would definitely go in the pro column. In fact everything about him was leading her to say yes. Before Burke, fun had been in very short supply.

He started the car and Syd paid attention to the sound of the engine, listening for a hesitation, miss or any sign of trouble. She heard none. That was disappointing because she would love an excuse to get her hands on the motor. It didn't take long to drive to her house and Burke stopped in the driveway behind her fuel-efficient compact car.

After turning off the ignition, he looked at her. "I think you should invite me in."

"For a nightcap?"

"For anything you want. An invitation would be much appreciated."

The innuendo raised tingles all over her body. "Would it now?"

I'm attracted to you.

The memory of his words kicked up her heart rate and made her pulse dance in the most exciting possible way.

"Yes, it would. Your father's not coming home."

If her dad hadn't announced his plans to the world she could have used his imminent return as an excuse. If she wanted one. But suddenly it was crystal clear that she wasn't ready for the evening to end.

"Would you like to come inside? For something?" Where in the world did that seductive tone come from?

"I thought you'd never ask."

He opened his door then came around to hers. She put her palm in the hand he held out and he steadied her as she slid out of the passenger seat. Then he walked her to the front door and took her key to unlock it.

Inside, she flipped the switch on the wall to illuminate the room before putting her evening bag and to-go box on the small table just inside the door. After that she stepped out of her four-inch heels. She'd barely turned toward him when Burke had her in his arms. He tilted his head to the side and lowered his mouth to hers.

Sydney sighed at the softness of his lips. Relief poured through her that he was doing exactly what she wanted. She nestled closer to his tall, lean body and slid her hands beneath his suit coat, working up his back. His shirt was soft to the touch and his muscles bunched and contracted under her hands.

He traced her lips with his tongue and she opened to him, savoring the heat that exploded in her belly when he dipped inside. The sound of their escalated breathing filled the room and fueled her need.

Burke lifted his head and met her gaze, his eyes searching. "Are you ready to give me an answer to my question now?"

He'd said he wanted to get to know her better and this definitely qualified, so count her in. It also answered her question about what he would do if they were alone, and she couldn't deny her willingness to participate. She wasn't sure why she'd stalled because he'd had her at flowers and dinner.

"Yes," she whispered.

"Yes, you have an answer? Or yes, you want to spend time with me?"

"Both."

She slid her hands up his chest to his shoulders and lifted his suit coat, dragging it down his arms before dropping it on the floor. Then she reached up and unknotted his tie, pulling one end hand over hand until it was free of his collar. With a twist of his fingers he undid the button at his throat and Syd helped with the rest marching down the front of his shirt.

When she tried to repeat the maneuver used in taking

off his coat, he captured her hands and kissed the knuckles of each before guiding them around his waist.

"My turn." He reached behind her and slowly dragged down the zipper on her dress.

Cool air rushed in, caressing her skin. She wasn't wearing a bra and if this dress came off she would have on nothing but black lace panties. Anticipation was building inside and her blood rushed through her veins. Roared in her ears.

There was a distant sound and it took several moments to realize it was Burke's cell. He pulled her close and said, "Ignore that. It can wait."

"Are you sure?" She looked up to see his expression. "It's just late enough not to be a good time for the phone to ring."

He hesitated a moment longer, then yanked the device from his pocket. The frown turned angry when he looked at the caller ID and hit talk. "What is it, Dad?"

He listened for several moments, his expression growing darker by the second. Finally he said, "I'll be there tomorrow."

Without another word he clicked off.

Syd struggled to clear her head and pull up the zipper on her dress. Something told her that whatever she'd agreed to by saying yes would have to wait. "What's wrong?"

"I have to go to Chicago." He took another step away and dragged his fingers through his hair.

"Is your father all right?"

"Fine." He practically snapped out the word. "It's Mary—the housekeeper. She's in the hospital. They're doing tests."

Mary was the woman who'd been with him since his son was a baby and obviously the news worried him. But it wasn't just that. "Where is Liam? Who's taking care of him?"

"My father." He didn't look happy about that. "I have to go."

"Of course. This will be scary for him."

He nodded grimly. "And staying with his grandfather isn't the best option. The old man isn't someone you can count on."

Syd was surprised at the hostility in his tone but didn't ask. Mostly it was none of her business and this wasn't the time for probing questions. "What are you going to do?"

It was obvious that his mind was racing, clicking through possible scenarios to problem-solve the situation. "Work is crazy now. The time frame for the resort is tight. I can't afford to be gone."

She remembered what he'd said about the boy's friends and activities being in Chicago. And that was why he'd opted not to bring him to Blackwater Lake, even for the end of summer. "Is there anyone else to take care of Liam?"

"No one I can think of. I would have to personally interview a replacement for Mary. But there's no time for that." He met her gaze. "Unless there's something I haven't thought of, Liam will have to come back here with me."

She could tell by the harried expression on his face that this wasn't the time to say that might not be such a bad thing.

Instead, she put her arms around his waist and rested her cheek against his chest. "I'm sorry this is happening."

"Me, too." He kissed the top of her head. "I apologize, but I have to go. Arrangements to make—"

"I understand." She gave him a reassuring smile. "Go do what you have to."

"I'll call you." He kissed her cheek, then let himself out the door.

Syd stared at it for a long time after he'd left and a number of things came to mind. Burke could have had his father put the boy on a plane to Montana. He hadn't and was personally going to get him. He could have had someone else interview a substitute housekeeper, but he wouldn't do that, either. To her way of thinking he'd handled this situation as a caring parent should.

And yet he didn't consider himself a good father. She was no shrink, but it was a good bet that core belief was rooted in his relationship with his own father. How she would love to hear that story and tell him he was very wrong about his parenting skills.

Chapter Eight

Burke was tired.

The last couple of days had been hectic and his surly eight-year-old didn't help. There'd been no choice but to bring Liam back to Blackwater Lake. He couldn't leave the boy with his grandfather. It was bad enough that the man had already screwed him up. If anyone was going to screw up Liam, Burke would do it.

He glanced over at the boy, sitting on the leather sofa in his office. It was in the five-story building Brady O'Keefe had built to house his company. O'Keefe Technology had four floors and rented out number five to Burke. When his cousin Sloan arrived he would need work space and as the resort project kicked into full gear, they'd need a place to put a lot of employees. So while this floor was pretty empty now, very soon it would be activity central.

He looked over at Liam again and the fierce frown on the kid's face made him feel as if he'd been smacked with the guilty stick. Obviously the boy was unhappy, but Burke hadn't done this on purpose. How could he make his child understand the situation?

Before he went crazy trying to answer that question his intercom buzzed. He hit the talk button and said, "Yes, Lydia?"

"There's someone here to see you."

"Thanks." Without saying anything else, he clicked off.

Normally he would have asked who was there or had them sent in. The fact that he didn't told Burke two things. Number one: he was grateful for the interruption. Number two: he needed a break. The electricity in this room was so thick you could charge a car battery with it.

He stood and walked around his desk. "There's someone here to see me, Liam."

"Yeah. I heard."

"I'll be right back."

The only response was a grunt; the kid didn't even look up from his handheld video game. Burke would have preferred he pick up the book sitting beside him but that was a battle for another day.

When he came out of his office, Lydia wasn't sitting at her desk.

"Sydney." He could truthfully say he'd never been so glad to see anyone in his life. It felt like years since he'd nearly taken her to bed. God, he'd regretted having to leave her that night.

"Lydia said to tell you she'll be right back. She went to the ladies' room," she said. "How are you?"

"Okay."

She was so beautiful, even dressed for work as she was now, although his favorite was the little black dress that he'd almost taken off her. But there was something about just looking at her that made him feel refreshed.

He walked over and kissed her. They were alone if you didn't count his son in the other room. But he didn't care who was or wasn't watching. He kissed her like a starving man and felt as if he couldn't get enough. A little moan escaped her lips and the sound of it set him on fire. But this was a place of business.

Forcing himself to pull away, he smiled down at her. "What are you doing here?"

"I heard you were back."

Her tone wasn't peeved or accusing, but he felt another slap with the guilty stick. "I'm sorry I didn't call. I know I promised, but it's been crazy—"

"I can imagine," she interrupted. "It's okay. I was just passing by and thought I'd stop in and say hi. Unless you're too busy."

"I am, but this is a good time for a break."

Her gaze was assessing. "You look tired. What happened with Liam?"

"He's in my office." He glanced past his executive assistant's desk to the partially opened door. "Mary is still in the hospital. She needs surgery."

"I hope it's not serious."

"When you're in your sixties any surgery is serious. The doctors say she'll be fine, but there will be recovery time." He rubbed a hand across the back of his neck, recalling the conversation that pulled the rug out from under him. "Bottom line is she's retiring. Effective immediately."

"Can she afford to?"

"I'll make sure of it. I owe her more than I can ever repay."

There was concern in her dark eyes. "What are you going to do?"

"Long-term I'm not sure. Short-term, I have to enroll him in school. I've filled out all the forms for Blackwater Lake Elementary, but they need his records from Chicago before he can start. It will be a couple of days so he's with me until that gets squared away."

"It must be nice to have him here."

"Yes. And no."

"How so?" she asked.

"He's been…difficult." Mouthy. Disrespectful. Stubborn. Rebellious. Those adjectives would work, too.

"Change is never easy." Her voice was soft, comforting. Consoling.

"I wish he didn't have to go through this. Liam is very close to Mary."

"It's tough. Unfortunately this is the stuff that builds character. But you already understand that, don't you?"

"I know how it feels to be on the receiving end of being told that everything is going to change."

"What happened?" Her eyes filled with sympathy.

"My mother got sick. Cancer. She died when I was a little older than Liam. It's hard for a kid to process something like this." He met her gaze. "On top of worrying about Mary, he didn't want to leave his friends and activities. Especially sports."

"There are organized sports for kids here in Blackwater Lake."

"As he pointed out school has started and teams have already been formed. He's right about that, but the timing of this makes him even more resentful."

"Give him time, Burke."

She put her hand on his forearm, the part where his rolled-up shirt sleeve left the skin bare. The touch, slight though it was, reassuring as it was meant to be, still sent the blood rushing to points south of his belt. He wanted her naked in his arms. And this wasn't the time or place to be thinking things like that. But it seemed he had little control over her effect on him.

"I don't have much choice," he said. "And in the meantime, I'm the only one he has to take his anger out on."

"Just talk to him. He's pretty young and won't understand, but he'll always remember that you were there for him when he was going through a rough patch."

The advice touched a nerve because that was his chief complaint about his own father. When his mom died, his dad seemed never to be home. Work was always more important than what was going on with Burke.

"Would you like to meet him? Unless you don't have time…"

"I'd love to."

He thought her reaction was sincere and said, "Okay, then. Follow me."

They walked over to the door and he pushed it open. "Hey, Liam, I'd like to introduce you to a friend of mine."

The boy glanced up, but the sullen expression didn't budge. There was only a small amount of satisfaction to be had from the fact that he wasn't the only target of his son's hostility.

"Liam, this is Sydney McKnight. Syd, my son, Liam."

She walked over and sat down beside him. "It's nice to meet you, Liam. Your dad has told me a lot about you."

"Yeah. Whatever."

Burke felt the simmering anger tighten inside him. "That's rude, son. I know Mary didn't teach you that kind of behavior."

"It's okay, Burke." Syd stared at the boy until he looked straight at her. "How do you like Blackwater Lake?"

"It's small and there's nothing to do here." He took a quick look around the office as if to say this was ground zero of boredom.

"It will be better when you start school," she told him.

"School here is probably small and boring, too." The childish tone was full to overflowing with contempt. "It doesn't matter anyway. I don't care."

Burke figured he could take whatever the boy dished out, but Sydney didn't need this. "Liam—"

The child stood and headed for the door. "I have to go to the bathroom."

When he was gone Burke blew out a long breath. "What a charmer."

"He takes after you," she teased.

"Wow, feel the love." He slid her a wry glance. "Seriously, Syd, I'm sorry about that. He has issues with me but normally he's polite to strangers."

"Don't worry about it. I'd be willing to bet that giant chip on his shoulder is all about being a scared kid whose whole world just turned upside down."

"I'd be glad if you're right because I pretty much decided it had more to do with him hating me."

"I'm sure that's not true," she said.

Burke figured she was wrong about that. He'd gone through a phase of not liking his own father very much. After Burke let go of any expectations for the old man, he and Walker Holden had reached a state of benign coexistence. They tolerated each other when necessary. His expectations of the relationship with his own son were higher than that, but it looked as if that was doomed to failure.

"Fingers crossed that you're right and going to school will help. By the way, I had to put down an emergency contact number and I gave them yours. I hope you don't mind."

"Not a problem. They probably won't need it but I'm happy to help if necessary. It's the way folks roll here in Blackwater Lake." She actually looked as if she meant what she'd said.

"Thanks." He glanced out to his assistant's desk. "Lydia's back. She's not going to like what I'm going to ask her to do."

"What's that?"

"I have a meeting this afternoon. It has to be canceled and rescheduled."

"Because of Liam. You can't take him with you?" she asked.

He shook his head. "A difficult eight-year-old would be a distraction. And I can't really blame him. If I had to listen to a bunch of grown-ups talking for hours, I'd be difficult, too."

"See? You get where he's coming from." She smiled at him, then stood and walked closer. "Your instincts are spot-on. You, sir, are your own worst critic."

"No. I think Liam takes first place on that."

She sighed. "My father always said it's in the rules and part of the job description that kids are going to give their parents a hard time." She tapped her lip. "And speaking of Dad, I just had an idea."

"About what?"

"How to not annoy your executive assistant." She met his gaze. "Liam doesn't want to be cooped up here. How about if I take him to the garage with me?"

"But you have to work. I couldn't ask you to do that."

"You didn't. I volunteered. And my dad won't mind. He always brought me there when I was a little girl. He managed to work with a child around."

"I don't know."

"We can find stuff to keep him busy, although, fair warning, he might get dirty."

"I don't care about that," he said.

"Then it's settled." During the short silence her eyes narrowed. "Unless you don't trust me."

"Of course I do. It just seems like an imposition."

"I would tell you if it was. Or I'd have kept my mouth shut and not offered in the first place."

Burke couldn't fault that reasoning and finally said, "Okay. Thanks. I don't know how I can repay you for this, but I really owe you."

"I'll think of something."

The saucy, suggestive look in her eyes heated his blood and threatened to fry his brain. He had some ideas that brought to mind twisted sheets and tangled legs, and fervently hoped what she thought of as payback would be along those lines.

"And who do we have here? Is this your young apprentice?"

Syd recognized her father's voice and the veiled reference to *Star Wars,* but was surprised that he'd managed to approach without her hearing. Looking down at Liam, who moved a little closer beside her, she figured that it was because she had a thing or two on her mind.

"Dad, this is Liam Holden, Burke's son. Liam, this is my father, Tom McKnight."

The little boy held out his hand and solemnly said, "How do you do, Mr. McKnight. It's nice to meet you."

"I didn't know Burke had a son." Her dad leaned over and shook hands then gave her a look that said this level of good manners and courtesy wasn't normal for a kid his age. "You're very polite, son."

"My dad told me I have to be."

"He's right." Her father nodded approvingly. "It sure helps smooth the way with people you meet."

"I guess." Liam lifted a thin shoulder.

"Welcome to Blackwater Lake, Liam. How do you like it so far?"

"Thank you, sir. And so far it's boring."

"I guess your dad told you to be honest, too," Tom said drily.

"Yes, sir." Liam glanced up at her. "But it's a little better since Sydney came to see my dad."

Tom looked at her, then the boy. "Ah."

"I stopped by Burke's office and offered to bring Liam over here. He's been very helpful. Watching and hand-ing me tools." If the dirt stains on the front of his shirt and pants were anything to go by, the kid was having the time of his life.

Her father's eyebrows lifted. "You know only employees are allowed in the service bay."

"That's why we're not in the service bay." The car was just outside with her rolling toolbox beside it. "It's a beautiful day so I pulled it out here to do the tune-up."

"I see."

She met his gaze and felt a compulsion to defend her actions, not unlike when she'd been a teenager. "The housekeeper who cares for Liam has suddenly taken ill and Burke brought him back to Blackwater Lake. He was cooped up in his father's office and bored to tears."

"I wasn't crying," Liam explained. "I'm not a crybaby."

"Of course you're not and I didn't mean to imply that. It's just an expression to explain how bored you actually were."

"Really bored," he said vehemently.

"Burke had a meeting this afternoon and he was going to cancel it. I figured helping out would be…helpful. Isn't that what folks here in Blackwater Lake do?"

"You're working, too," her father pointed out, ignoring the question.

"But my job is different. It's more flexible. And fun."

"This is an awesome place, Mr. McKnight."

"Call me Tom."

"Yes, sir. I mean Tom," Liam said.

Syd knew her father and knew by the expression on his face that he was struggling with something. Part of it could be that she hadn't told him Burke had a child.

Finally he said to the boy, "Would you like a soda, Liam?"

"Dad," she interjected, "I don't know if soda is the best drink—" The warning look in his eyes made her stop talking. Funny how he could still do that even though she was all grown up.

"It won't hurt him. You used to have one almost every day after school."

"Sydney got to come here when she was a kid?" Liam's tone said that had to be on a par with going to an amusement park. When her father nodded, he said, "Cool."

"So, Liam, would you like something to drink?"

"That would be awesome."

"Okay. Let's go to my office."

After they left, she started a visual inspection beneath the hood of the car. She checked the drive and serpentine belts. They looked loose and would need adjustment so she turned her attention to the tension pulleys.

She could do this in her sleep and her mind wandered while she worked. Something about the little boy tugged at her heart. He was the spitting image of Burke—brown hair, blue eyes and a smile that would melt a woman's heart. In about ten years he was going to be pretty hard for girls to resist.

The fact that he favored his father gave her a sense of poetic justice on Burke's behalf. It would have been so wrong for this boy to take after the woman who'd walked out and didn't fight for custody.

The same woman who had made Burke anti-marriage and children. That was just a darn shame because the man had a lot to offer a woman.

In hindsight, she realized it probably wasn't the smartest move to go see him, but her car kind of steered its way over. When it was time for the next service on her vehicle, she'd be sure to check that out. Curiosity was annoying and inconvenient, but also a powerful motivator. After not hearing from him, she just had to find out how things were going and it was a good thing she had. They'd barely walked out of Burke's office and the kid's hostile attitude disappeared. Maybe the two Holden men being stuck with each other for a while was a blessing in disguise, forcing them to work through their issues.

Behind her she heard footsteps and voices. As the older man and young boy walked toward her, she smiled. Her dad had a way with kids and Liam looked completely comfortable, chatting away as if he'd known Tom McKnight for years instead of minutes. He had a soda in one hand and two small cars in the other.

"Where'd you get those?" she asked, nodding at the toys.

"One was Alex's and the other Ben's. The boys used to play with them here when your mother needed the afternoon for errands or just some time off to recharge her battery." He smiled at the pun.

"I'm surprised you still have them," she said, a lump in her throat.

Her dad shrugged. "I just found them in a drawer."

Right, and she was the princess of an exotic foreign country. The man didn't like clutter and cleaned out on a regular basis. He'd kept these two toy cars for sentimental reasons and she loved him for it.

"You're a big softie."

Liam looked up at her. "Your dad said you didn't like toy cars. You wanted to play with the real thing."

"That's true," she confirmed. "Do you like cars, Liam?"

"Yeah." He glanced up at her father, the beginnings of hero worship in his eyes. "Tom said he would let me look at an engine. And touch it."

"That old one out back that you used to practice on when you were a kid," her dad clarified. "A little hands-on experience."

There was no reason to keep that old hunk of metal except as another sentimental gesture. With a heart that soft, no wonder he'd grieved the loss of his wife for so long.

She crouched down in front of Liam. "Is that what you want to do?"

"Yeah." Blue eyes so like his father's were bright with excitement.

"Okay." She should have thought of that. Rookie mistake. Pulling the rag from her back pocket, she started to wipe her hands. "I'll take you back there—"

"No need. Finish what you're doing. I'll take him." His eyes twinkled. "I miss having a young apprentice."

She said it again. "You're just a big softie."

"If that information gets around, I'll know who spread the rumor," he teased. "And I'll deny everything."

"I've got a news flash for you, big guy." Syd stood on tiptoe and kissed his cheek. "It's not a secret."

"Remind me to have a word with your brothers about that." He dropped a big hand on the small shoulder. "Come along, Liam."

"Do we need tools or anything?" Liam's expression was full of awe, with a dash of excitement mixed in for good measure. "Sydney has a whole bunch of them in that big red box with the wheels on it."

"No tools yet," her dad explained. "At first you just have to look and learn the names of everything."

"Will you teach me?"

"Sure."

The two walked around the service bay building and disappeared. The sight of her father taking the young boy under his wing brought back so many memories of hanging out here when she was little. Either school had been out and there was no child care. Or the babysitter got sick. Whatever the reason, when she had no place to go and no one to keep an eye on her she'd come to McKnight Automotive. Her father was her hero and she'd wanted to do what he did.

Until now it had never occurred to her how complicated

raising a little girl without a mother could be. When her brothers were little, her mother had been around. Losing her when his daughter was born had to have been so hard on her dad. Harder than Syd could even imagine. Bringing a new baby into the world should have been a happy event, but when you lost the love of your life that would leave a mark on the soul.

The realization made her more determined than ever to make sure her dad got his second chance at happiness. If that required a little subterfuge then so be it.

Whatever the circumstances, being a single parent was a lot harder than she'd ever thought and Burke was struggling with it. She'd been lucky to live in Blackwater Lake, where neighbors stepped in to lend a hand.

He wasn't staying, but he was here now. And she would help him.

Chapter Nine

A few days after meeting Liam and bringing him to work, Sydney got a call from Burke. The good news was the kid was finally in school. The bad news: there was an emergency. Burke was tied up in a permit meeting, an emergency of his own. He asked if there was any way she could pick up the boy, and promised to get away as soon as possible. Although she would have done it anyway, the worry and stress in his voice made her feel sorry for him and convinced her to help out.

She let her dad know what was going on and headed over to Blackwater Lake Elementary, which was about ten minutes beyond the garage on the north side of town. After parking in the lot, she headed up the sidewalk, past the flagpole and into the office at the front of the school.

It hadn't changed much since she'd been a student there. Blue industrial-strength carpet, pale yellow walls and the tall information desk that didn't seem quite as tall as it had when she'd been a student here.

Liam was sitting on the orange plastic seat of a chair against the wall. Another boy was there, too, with a chair between them. He was about the same age and looked familiar.

"May I help you?" There was a middle-aged woman standing behind the desk.

"Yes. I'm Sydney McKnight. I'm the emergency contact for Liam Holden."

"I talked to his father." The woman nodded. "There's been an incident—"

The office door opened behind her and Syd turned to see who it was. Violet walked in, looked at the boys, then noticed Syd standing there. She came over to the desk.

"Hi, Cheryl. I got a call about Todd."

"Yes. I was just about to explain the situation to Sydney."

"Why?"

"She's the emergency contact for the other boy involved. Burke Holden is his father."

"The multibazillionaire who's building the resort?"

"That's the one," Cheryl confirmed. "Anyway, Todd and Liam were fighting at recess. Blackwater Lake Elementary has a zero-tolerance policy about that sort of thing."

"Did Todd start it?" Violet asked.

Before the woman could answer Sydney said, "Doesn't matter. They both get sent home."

"That's right," the woman confirmed.

Violet looked surprised. "How did you know?"

"Because I'm sure things haven't changed and I have brothers. I bet your sisters never got sent home for fighting on the playground."

"You'd win that bet." She turned to glance at her son. "This is a new experience for me."

"The boys can come back tomorrow," Cheryl said. "And

hopefully with the time to think about this, their attitudes will have improved."

"So we're finished here?" Syd asked.

"Yes."

"Okay." She turned to Liam, who didn't appear especially combative. He looked small, a little scared and a lot sorry. "Let's go, kiddo."

Violet walked over to her blond, blue-eyed son. "Come on, Todd."

The boys picked up their backpacks and the four of them walked outside.

When they got to the sidewalk beside the flagpole, Syd put her hand on Liam's shoulder and stopped. "Do you want to tell me what happened?"

"No."

Violet coughed and Syd didn't dare look at her because she knew that was an attempt to cover a laugh. Syd had walked right into that one. Of course he didn't *want* to tell her what went on.

"It's almost lunchtime." Violet was checking her watch. "What do you say we sort this out over burgers and fries at the diner? I have to tell my boss why I'll be a little late for my shift anyway."

"Why?" Syd asked.

The other woman looked at her son. "I didn't plan on needing child care this early in the day. When I'm working, a high school girl comes over and is there to meet the kids when they get home from school. She gets them snacks and supervises homework until Charlie gets off work."

"I see."

She thought over the idea of lunch and remembered once asking her dad why he always took her brothers out to eat when they were in trouble. His answer: he had them for at least an hour and they had to talk. Usually he got useful information. The wisdom of it had never been clear to her until now.

"Okay," she said to Violet. "The diner it is."

They separated and took their respective vehicles into town and parked in the rear lot behind the Grizzly Bear Diner. After going inside Violet arranged for a table then talked to Michelle Crawford about her predicament. Syd texted Burke that she had Liam and let him know where they were. In a few minutes Violet joined them at a booth in the back and took the vacant seat beside her son.

"I have the best boss in the world."

"She has three grown sons," Syd pointed out wryly. "I guess it's all sorted out?"

"Yeah. I can keep Todd here with me for the lunch shift, then run him home when the sitter's there."

"I'm not a baby." Todd's tone was defensive and resentful.

"You're right," his mom said. "And your dad and I have raised you to use words. Hitting someone is never okay."

"Dad said I should defend myself if someone is picking on me."

Syd stared at Liam. She didn't know him well but he seemed like a sweet kid going through a difficult time, not a bully. "Were you picking on Todd?"

"No." The single word was defensive and resentful. The two boys were obstinate and hostile.

"Hi, Vi." The waitress—her name tag said Carla—came over to the table to take their orders. "What can I get you?"

When asked what they wanted the boys both lifted their shoulders in a shrug. Syd and Violet exchanged a glance then agreed on two Mama Bear combos and two Bear Cub combos that consisted of chicken nuggets, fries and a soft drink.

When they were alone again Violet said, "Liam is new

in town, Todd. In Blackwater Lake we make people feel welcome."

"I wasn't mean," he protested.

Syd had a feeling any blame for the altercation could be shared equally and in the spirit of peace negotiations it might be best not to single either of them out.

"You know," she said, "sometimes stuff just happens and gets out of hand. I think the school sends everyone involved home to think about it and figure out how to handle things differently in the future." She glanced at Violet, who nodded slightly.

"Sydney's right. This was a learning experience that you didn't have to get sitting at a desk in the classroom. A teachable moment."

"Does that mean we have homework?" Todd's expression was supposed to be innocent, but smacked of nine-year-old sarcasm.

Liam snickered. "That was a good one."

And the tension was broken. Todd pulled a couple of superhero action figures from his backpack, which seemed to surprise his mother—the toys probably shouldn't have been taken to school. A talk for another time. The boys each took a figure and started fake fighting with them, reaching across the table.

"I see the potential spilling hazards of this," Violet said. "But I don't have the heart to break this up. They're getting along. Talking."

"Like us." Syd smiled.

"Yeah. Who'd have thought?"

"You know I realized something after you brought your car into the shop." Syd unrolled silverware from her paper napkin and checked out the boys who were paying no attention to the adults. Still, she lowered her voice. "I was never in love with Charlie. We became a habit, not a couple."

"How do you know?" Violet looked surprised at the admission. "It's been ten years. Maybe you're just over it?"

She shook her head. "Memories came back when we talked. And a little while ago outside school I knew you were trying not to laugh when I asked if Liam *wanted* to tell me what happened. It hit me. After you guys left, I missed you. I was mourning the loss of my best friend."

There were tears in Violet's eyes when she reached across the table to grab Syd's hand. "I missed you, too."

"I'm glad you're here. I'm glad you moved back. I look forward to having my best friend around again."

"I look forward to that, too."

The food came then and they all dug in. With the air cleared all around, it seemed everyone was ravenous. A weight lifted from Syd's shoulders that might not have if she hadn't been Burke's emergency contact. This lunch was a good move, for her and Violet and the boys, too. Not unexpectedly, they finished first.

"Mom, I have to go to the bathroom."

"Me, too," Liam said.

Syd and Violet slid from the booth, letting the boys out. One of them said, "Race you," and the two took off.

"I was going to tell them no water fights," Syd said, "but I didn't want to give them any ideas."

"You have good mom instincts." Violet dragged a French fry through ketchup.

"I consider that a compliment. It has to be said that you handled this thing at school really well. No freaking out or overreacting. So calm and common sense."

"Thanks." Vi got a look on her face, a tell that personal questions were coming. "So, you're the emergency contact for Burke Holden's son."

"Yeah."

"C'mon, Syd. Give. Details. What's the story?"

"We're friends." She shrugged. "He asked, and like you

told Todd, folks in Blackwater Lake try to make newcomers feel welcome."

"I know you, Syd." Violet's eyes narrowed. "There's something you're not saying."

There were a lot of things she wasn't saying and didn't plan to. It was tempting to talk to her friend and share everything like she used to. But in this situation she couldn't. Not that Violet would spill the beans, but it could get awkward for her. Syd didn't want to put their newly repaired friendship in jeopardy.

Before she could answer, she saw Burke enter the diner, look around and head in her direction. He stopped at the end of their booth and she thought her heart would jump right out of her chest. This was unexpected and she was really happy to see him. Too happy for her peace of mind.

"I got here as soon as I could. What happened? Where's Liam?"

"In the restroom," Syd said. Then she proceeded to explain about the fight and the fact that the boys had worked out their differences. There was nothing to worry about.

"I'm really sorry to involve you, Syd," he said. "And Violet, I apologize if my son caused you any trouble. It won't happen again."

She laughed. "I appreciate that, but I won't hold you to it. Kids are unpredictable. On the upside, stuff blows over pretty quickly. Don't worry about this."

"That's very generous of you." He looked at Syd. "When I made you my emergency contact, I never dreamed that I'd really have to take you up on it. Liam will have consequences for this behavior, I assure you. I'm thinking in terms of grounding him for the rest of his life."

"I think a father-son talk might do more good," she suggested. "He's been yanked out of his comfort zone and is probably reacting to that. Besides, he and Todd seem to have made peace."

"And dare I say it?" Violet asked. "Maybe a friendship is budding?"

"That would be great." He looked at each of them. "As a gesture of goodwill, I took care of the lunch check."

"Very generous of *you*. Have you eaten yet?" Violet's tone was full of questions that had nothing to do with his lunch and everything to do with Syd and any relationship she might have with the handsome hotshot businessman. When he shook his head, she said, "Please join us. But before you do, it has to be said that the boys have been in the bathroom longer than seems necessary. We need a man to go in there and make sure there are no water fights going on."

"I can do that." He smiled at each of them. "Back in a minute."

"He's cute," Violet commented when he was out of earshot. "How did you meet him?"

"He brought his car in to the shop for an oil change." That was absolutely true. "And then things took off from there."

And how.

Burke had said he liked her and would have gotten around to dating her on his own. Maybe that was the truth. Maybe it wasn't. But they were after different things from a relationship. He didn't want more children and that was a deal breaker for her. As far as she could see, there was no way to negotiate a compromise.

As far as she was concerned it would be better if he stuck to her proposal. That would be the decent thing to do.

On the drive back to work Syd had some time to think. Violet deeply regretted the way she'd handled falling in love with Charlie—she really was sorry about not being honest with Syd right from the start. Making peace with

Violet was a relief and that realization made the burden of deceiving her father even more troublesome.

She pulled in to the automotive lot and parked her car, then went straight to the main office, where her dad was behind his flat-topped metal desk doing computer work. Before she could say anything, he glanced up and something about his expression reminded her of being sixteen years old and waiting for a boy to pick her up. He was troubled about something.

"How did things work out with Liam?" Tom's voice was soft and even, as if he was trying too hard to appear unconcerned.

"He's suspended from school for the rest of the day. Fighting." She slid her hands into the pockets of her work pants. "Coincidentally, the other boy involved was Violet's son, Todd. We took them to lunch. Violet's idea, actually. But I remembered how you used to do that with Alex and Ben when they were in some kind of trouble."

She was talking too much, a sure sign of being nervous. It wasn't easy, but she forced herself to shut up.

Even her compliment didn't coax a smile from her father. "That's good it all worked out."

"What's wrong, Dad?" When he opened his mouth to protest, she held up her hand to stop what she knew was coming. "Save it. I know when something's bothering you, so get it off your chest."

"You're not going to like it."

"Probably not. So let's get this over with."

"I'm uneasy about your relationship with Burke."

"But I thought you wanted me to be involved with someone," she protested.

"He's not from around here."

Even though she and Burke didn't have a real relationship, Syd felt compelled to argue that statement as a cause for concern. "You're nervous because he's an outsider? Seriously?"

"Yes." He leaned back in his chair and linked his fingers, then rested his hands over his flat belly.

She could see stubbornness move across his face and set up camp. "This is where I point out that Alex and Ben both married women who aren't from around here. Jill Beck Stone married a doctor who moved here from Las Vegas. They're all happy couples and starting families. What makes you think that just because Burke is from somewhere else that he's unworthy?"

Syd actually knew the answer. That part about starting a family wasn't going to happen with Burke. But she met her father's gaze, refusing to look away.

"He's temporary, Syd. His business is based somewhere else. He's here to get the resort going and then he'll go back where he came from." He sat forward and rested his forearms on the desk. "Plus he's got a son. Seems like a nice enough boy, but the fighting at school is a concern. He could be trouble."

"Oh, come on, Dad. Alex and Ben were no angels at Liam's age. They had skirmishes at school when they were kids. And you're their father. Does that mean you're not a suitable man to date?"

"We're not talking about me. This is about you settling down, so—"

"So that you can move on with your life and be happy. I get it." She had to tell him the truth and this was the time. "About that, Dad. I have something to say and you're not going to like it."

"Okay."

"Burke isn't really my boyfriend."

Although Burke had kissed her as if he was and she'd kissed him back. She really liked kissing him and had been prepared to sleep with him before he got the call about his housekeeper. Syd knew her willingness to go to bed with the man colored everything a murky shade of gray. Technically he wasn't her boyfriend but he had said he wanted to date her. Casually. So she wasn't exactly sure what they were.

Her dad rubbed a hand across his face. "So when he drove in here and you introduced him as the guy you'd been seeing, that was a lie?"

"A big, hairy one," she confirmed. "But, in my own defense—wrong thing, right reason."

"That reason being an attempt to get me to commit to Loretta?"

"Yes. You have to admit you're practically living with the mayor. Isn't it about time you get her a ring? Make an honest woman of her?" Syd hoped now he really was in a place where he could hear her.

His mouth twitched, evidence that he was trying to maintain a stern face and failing big-time. "So you think we should get hitched?"

"Although that term brings to mind a horse attached to a wagon, if you're as smart as I think you are, you'll propose and get married as soon as possible." Syd moved closer to the desk and settled her hip on the corner. "You deserve to have all the good things in life. I hope you know that. You have to squeeze the happy out of every single day."

"I do know that."

"Then get off your tush and quit wasting time." Emotion and her passion to make him understand kicked up the pitch of her voice. "I can take care of myself. And if I need help, which I won't, isn't it better for me to have you and Loretta together? The way I see it, you're a twofer."

A slow smile curved his mouth. "That's a nice thing to say."

"I'm a nice person." She grinned. "So now I have to come up with your power-couple nickname."

"What in the world?"

"They do that with Hollywood couples. Combine first names. You and Loretta could be Lo-Tom. Or my personal favorite, drumroll please—Tom-Lo."

"Stop." He shook a finger at her, then turned serious. "Syd, thank you for trusting me with the truth."

"Actually, I really hate deceiving you. Too much guilt to carry around."

"And I have to confess that I didn't really buy the act. It was suspicious from the start."

"I guess it's a compliment that I'm not a very good liar." She folded her arms over her chest, not really surprised by his admission. As a kid, she could never pull a fast one without him being wise to it. "And in the spirit of full disclosure, the whole truth is that the day he drove in, I'd never seen him before in my life. But we spent time together pretending to be a couple."

"And you like him." It wasn't a question.

She nodded. "And he says he likes me. That he'd have gotten around to asking me out sooner or later."

Just thinking about the look in his eyes when he'd said that made her quiver all over. The attention, especially from a man like him, was incredibly flattering and that was a problem. It could set her up for a really hard fall.

"I see." Her father nodded thoughtfully. "It goes without saying that he has excellent taste. But, Syd, I can't help having concerns—"

"Objections," she interrupted.

"That's too strong a word. He seems like a nice enough guy. I don't think he would deliberately hurt you, but my concerns about the two of you haven't changed. He's an outsider and unlikely to stay here in Blackwater Lake."

"Understood."

"Syd—" He got to his feet and said her name to stop her from leaving when she straightened away from the desk. "Before you go—I have to apologize. I didn't mean to push you into lying about your personal life. I've only ever wanted to be a good father. Protect you."

"Oh, Dad—" She walked over and gave him a hug. "You're an amazing father."

"I wouldn't go that far."

"I would," she said eagerly. "Watching you with Liam reminded me of when I was a little girl and how much I loved hanging out with you." She stepped back and smiled up at him. "Still do. Thanks for being the best father I could ask for."

"Thank you for loving me enough to do anything for my happiness."

"If you don't ask Loretta soon, I may have to get really creative and wild. Who knows what I'll do?"

"Now you're starting to scare me. I promise I'll take care of it." His voice was teasing, before his expression turned serious. "But do me a favor, Syd. Don't get hurt."

"No need to worry, Dad. I've got it under control." So she'd just told another lie.

The truth was she'd never felt about anyone the way she did about Burke. It was dishonest to say she had everything under control when every time he walked into a room she had less power over her feelings. All she had for sure was a bucketload of doubts.

Chapter Ten

"Thanks for meeting me here, Syd." Burke held out a hand indicating one of the visitor chairs in front of his desk. "I have a favor to ask."

"Another one?" Her smile was teasing.

He really liked that smile. It felt like forever since he'd seen her, but just the day before he'd had lunch at the diner while Sydney, Violet and the boys kept him company. The whole experience had felt so completely normal and fun. He hadn't wanted to go back to the office and that was saying something for a man whose life was his work.

Today he'd asked her to come to the office when she left McKnight Automotive. Since she was busy when he'd called, there wasn't a chance to explain why he wanted to see her. But she wasn't wearing McKnight Automotive standard-issue pants and shirt, which indicated she'd taken the time to change. Her fashion instincts were spot-on. She looked chic and beautiful in straight-leg jeans, a white silk blouse, a navy blazer and low-heeled shoes.

"I hate to impose on you again," he said. "It isn't enough that you helped me out with the fighting incident at school yesterday. Believe me I'm grateful."

"And your way of paying me back is asking for more? You really were born with a silver spoon in your mouth, weren't you?" she teased.

Burke shrugged. It was a blessing and curse. Money didn't make your life perfect. If so, his mother wouldn't have died so young. On paper, a guy who'd grown up without a mom and was raised by his father should have been equipped to parent his own son whose mother had no interest in the job. But Burke's father had never been around and he had no blueprint for how to be a dad. Syd, on the other hand, had never even known her mother but had hit the dad jackpot. From him she'd absorbed great instincts.

"Before I get to the favor, I have to tell you that Liam and I had a greeting-card moment last night. Thanks to you."

"Really? What did I do?"

"You suggested a father-son chat instead of grounding him for eternity."

"Oh, that."

"Yes. That." He leaned forward, forearms on the desk. "I told him I wanted to talk about what happened at school. He was sullen and defensive at first, but eventually he opened up. It was—" He stopped, searching for the right description and finally said, "A first for us."

She looked pleased. "What did he say?"

"That everything's different here and he doesn't like it. He's angry and feeling insecure."

"He said that?" she asked, obviously surprised. "Awfully grown up."

"Not in those exact words, but the message came through. It's not home, not what he's used to."

"How can it be when this is only temporary?" She

shrugged, but that didn't distract from the shadows in her eyes.

Burke had a feeling something was bothering her and didn't like it. He preferred her sunny-side up and wanted to fix any problem. That was new, he realized. Usually when a woman needed something emotional fixed, he headed for the nearest exit.

"What's wrong?" he asked.

Her lips compressed into a tight line. "If you hadn't called me, I was going to call you."

He was glad to hear that, although her expression was a clue that her motivation wasn't necessarily similar to his. The favor he wanted to ask was a thinly veiled excuse to see her. One thing he'd learned since bringing his son to live with him—when a single father didn't have live-in child care, dating was complicated. He had to get creative.

"Why were you going to call me?" he asked.

"To let you know we don't have to fake it any more. Dad knows what I did."

By that Burke was pretty sure she meant that their relationship deal was outed. But the truth was that after the first dinner with Syd and her dad, he hadn't been pretending to like her.

Which begged the question… "How did he find out?"

"I confessed." She shrugged again. "I couldn't keep lying to him."

"How did he take it?" Burke liked Tom McKnight and losing the man's favorable opinion bothered him. "Was he angry?"

"No. And that's the worst part. If he'd gotten mad, I could have been defensive and self-righteous. This was so much worse." She shook her head at the memory. "He said he's just trying to be a good father. Protect me."

Burke shared the man's inclination for that and could understand the motivation for putting off his own life for the sake of his child. But he could also understand Syd's determination to convince her dad she was okay and get him to commit to a new, personal phase.

"Should I talk to him?" he offered.

"Why would you want to?" She seemed surprised by that.

"Because I don't want him to think I make a habit of deceiving people."

She tilted her head to study him. "You actually care what he thinks of you."

"Yes." Now he shrugged.

"It would be very noble of you and I have no objection. For the record, he claims he wasn't fooled for a second." She shifted in the chair. "In the spirit of complete honesty, I did tell him what you said, that you'd have gotten around to asking me out if I hadn't approached you first."

"So you told him everything?"

"Pretty much." Her expression was guarded, indicating she'd held something back.

He decided it best not to push. "So I can make an honest woman of you now?"

"Others have tried and failed," she joked. "So, don't keep me in suspense. What is this favor? Just so you know, I'm keeping a tab."

"I wouldn't have it any other way." He grinned and leaned back in his chair. "The idea actually came from my talk with Liam. It was his anger and insecurity that made me call you today."

"Interesting. My expertise is with a car engine. I'm not a shrink."

"Very funny." This is where he had to sell the idea. "This is much easier than that. You're a local. I have an appointment with a real-estate agent who also manages rentals in and around Blackwater Lake."

"Okay." A puzzled look crossed her face. "I'm not sure how I can help with that."

"The thing is, I think if I can find a house to rent, something more homey than the lodge, it might help Liam to feel settled. I guess it's a dad thing."

"I think it's a good idea. But I still don't know what I can do to make it easier."

"That's where being a local comes in. I need your advice on location, good or bad, and your general impression of the property. From a woman's perspective."

"Well, I'm a woman."

And how. Burke couldn't help it when his gaze dropped from her eyes to the top button on that silky blouse. She *was* a woman and he was the guy who almost had her. If only his cell phone had rung *after* they'd let nature take its course maybe he wouldn't ache to touch her now. And now was a lot more complicated than then.

"All I'm asking for is your educated opinion on what we see today."

She nodded. "No one ever said I don't have opinions. I can do that."

"Great." He stood. "We're picking Liam up at Todd's house on the way to meet the agent at the first property. I have the list he emailed."

She smiled. "Liam had a playdate?"

"Yeah. Progress. And if he's going to reciprocate, it would be nice to have a house to do it in. Not a hotel." He looked at her. "Let's go."

Several hours later, the three of them had racked up more frustration than miles. There hadn't been much to look at and for what they'd seen, the agent had used adjectives and descriptions like *rugged. Rustic. Diamond-in-the-rough.* Something a splash of TLC would fix right up.

After Burke had declined all of the rentals, they'd

gone back to his office so she could pick up her car. The Holdens' collective discouragement was too much. Syd had invited father and son to her house for dinner. She didn't have the heart to send them back to Blackwater Lake Lodge. As nice as her sister-in-law, Cam, made the place, it wasn't a home. The least she could do was not condemn them to another meal in a restaurant. She offered to fix a home-cooked meal for the boys.

And if she was being honest, with her dad spending all his free time with Loretta, Syd was a little lonely eating by herself.

She and Burke were sitting outside in patio chairs at the round table that could accommodate four. They were sipping white wine while Liam kicked around an old soccer ball that had once belonged to one of her brothers. Glancing over, she noted that Burke's expression was troubled. Being unable to make a home happen for his son had to be really hard for a man used to holding power and getting what he wanted. Or making it happen.

"The first place wasn't that bad," she said, trying to cheer him up.

When he met her gaze, his was wry. "If you like sharing your living space with a raccoon family."

"You don't know animals were occupying it. That was the agent's speculation."

"More like an educated guess. Based on the fact that the cabinets were rifled through and the place was trashed. Looked like wolves lived there."

"Maybe Mr. and Mrs. Raccoon had a party and invited friends." She sipped her wine, then said, "I know, maybe it was the kids. The folks were out hunting and gathering while the teenagers threw a kegger without permission."

One corner of his mouth curved up. "Nice try."

"I thought it was pretty good, actually. I can only conclude that you're determined to pout."

"When you put it like that…" He was slumped in the chair, head resting on the thick outdoor pad. His gaze followed his son, running around chasing the black-and-white ball. "Look how much he's enjoying being outside. I don't think Cam would sanction him practicing headers and goal kicks in our suite at the lodge."

"I would put in a good word, but you're probably right about that." Syd laughed. "But it's not the end of the world. You have four walls and a roof over your head. A two-bedroom suite. Best in town."

"And it's lovely." He rolled his head to the side and glanced at her. "Can I just say that this resort can't be built too soon. Blackwater Lake needs more housing options."

"I can see why you'd think so."

"If only I didn't have to be here, but I've found that things go a lot faster and smoother if I'm on site from the beginning, meeting face-to-face with people, keeping everyone accountable for the work. Flying back and forth to troubleshoot really slows things down."

She nodded. "I see your point."

"For the record," he said, "I'm not pouting. Just disappointed."

Liam kicked the ball toward where they were sitting then flopped in the chair beside his father's. He took a sip from the glass of lemonade in front of him. "What are we gonna do, Dad?"

"About what?"

"A place to live."

"It would appear that we have no choice but to stay where we are, son."

"Really? No way. Todd lives in a nice house and has a really big backyard. We played tag today with his little sister. She was 'it' all the time 'cuz we were faster."

Syd wasn't sure how that information was connected

to the current problem, but figured all would be revealed. "Sounds like you had fun today."

"Yeah." He looked at his father. "But you always say when you get invited somewhere you should invite them back. How can I do that? We can't play tag in a hotel."

Burke's mouth pulled tight. "We'll think of some way to reciprocate."

"What?" Liam rubbed a knuckle under his nose.

"Return the favor," Burke explained.

"I don't see how." He slumped in his chair and looked like Burke's Mini-Me. "I'm the only kid in my class who lives in a hotel."

"Technically, it's a lodge," Syd said. "And have you asked everyone in the class where they live?"

"No." Liam thought for a moment. "But I haven't seen any of them at the lodge. And I would have if they lived there."

"Good point." She met Burke's gaze and whispered, "I think he's going to be a lawyer when he grows up."

That got a grin, but it faded fast. Syd could see that it was killing him not to be able to give his son what he wanted most and blamed himself for the fact that he couldn't. She fully expected his next words to be about a trip to the toy store—to buy something to make him feel better. But his comment surprised her.

"I'm bummed about the situation, too, Liam. But there's not really anything I can do to change it. We're lucky to have a nice place to live and enough food to eat. There are a lot of people in the world who don't have that."

"Yeah, I know. That doesn't mean it doesn't stink."

"I hear you, buddy."

"You know, Liam," she said, "if you want to be out-side with friends, there's the park. It's brand-new—just opened officially a few weeks ago." One of her first very public "dates" with Burke. "There's lots of room to run and

fun equipment to play on. Or you could come over here."
She held out a hand, indicating all the space available for
running and playing. "This is a big yard and my dad still
has my brothers' basketball and portable hoop, baseball
and mitt. Lots of stuff to use outdoors. You're welcome
to come over anytime."

"Really?" Blue eyes so like his father's glowed with
excitement.

"Really. *Mi casa, su casa.* And, before you ask, that's
Spanish for my house is your house. Just give me a call
before you come over. Okay?"

"Awesome! Thanks, Syd."

"You're welcome."

"I'm going to practice soccer again. It would be more
fun if Todd was here, though."

"We'll work on making that happen," Syd promised.

"Cool." Liam stood, then walked over, leaned down
and hugged her. "Thanks."

"You're welcome." She smiled, marveling at the abundance of youthful energy as he kicked the ball nearly to
the back fence and ran after it.

"Yeah, thanks," Burke echoed. "I owe you. Again. It
seems my debt to you just keeps growing, a helping-hand
tab."

"No big deal. It's like you said about returning favors.
Paying it forward. When my dad needed help, folks were
there. It's the Blackwater Lake way."

"And this town is a great place. But—" He reached over
and linked his fingers with hers. "I can't think of anyone
I would rather be in debt to."

Oh, my. The warmth of his hand made her tingle and the
heated look in his eyes had her wishing they were alone.
This presented her with a dilemma. Her dad knew the truth
about them pretending to be an item. Burke knew her dad

knew so there was no reason for pretense, no need to act as if they were attracted. Unless they really were attracted.

He was voluntarily holding her hand and looking at her as if he wanted to take her upstairs and ravage her. And she would very much like to be ravaged by Burke Holden.

But…how she hated that word. She also felt a swell of contentment. A peek into what it would be like to have a family of her own.

And that was a problem.

Sex was a purely biological need. But if the physical need became an emotional attachment, then things dipped into dangerous territory.

The conversation with her friend Maggie echoed her father's concerns. Burke didn't live in Blackwater Lake. This was all temporary, with very little chance of working out in the long run. She had to keep her heart out of the equation, keep it from getting crushed.

It had happened once and even though that was a long time ago, a girl didn't ever forget how bad it felt. This was not a good time to remember that distance from Burke was what she needed. Unfortunately she'd just offered him her house as a playground.

About five minutes after Burke and Liam left Syd was still putting the finishing touches on cleaning up the kitchen. Hamburgers and paper plates didn't make a big mess, but the sink needed a scrub and the granite counters could use a wiping down. She heard the sound of the front door opening and closing, followed by her father walking into the kitchen. He was holding the soccer ball in his hands.

"Don't tell me. This is a clue that you're leaving the family business to train for the women's World Cup."

"Very funny." She folded up the dishrag and settled it over the hump between the two sinks. "You just missed

Burke and Liam. I invited them over for dinner and got out the ball for the kid. He needed to run around."

"I see."

Syd hated when her father said that. It sounded so relaxed, rational and reasonable, but she knew it really meant he didn't see at all. The words didn't quite take on the impact of disapproval because the tone wasn't there. But it was awfully close.

As always happened, those two one-syllable words goaded her into an attempt to change his attitude. "Burke asked me to go with them to look at rental houses. Now that his son is here with him, he'd like to get out of the lodge and into something more family-oriented."

"How'd that go?" Her dad tucked the ball underneath his arm, then leaned back against the island across from her.

"You know as well as I do that there's very little for lease around here that's decent and available. It was a complete bust."

"You felt bad and asked them to stay for dinner."

She shouldn't be surprised that he knew her so well, but somehow she was. "Yeah. Liam needed to let off some steam, get rid of that energy."

"I see."

There it was again. That response was starting to make her teeth hurt. She might as well put everything out there, including the standing invitation she'd initiated.

"I told them that any time he needed a yard to play in ours was available."

"What about the park?" Her father's voice was pleasant, the tone unchanged. His expression gave no clue about what he was thinking.

"I mentioned it."

Tom nodded thoughtfully. "That's nice of you to offer our yard."

"But?"

He shook his head. "But nothing. It was a really nice gesture on your part."

"But…you're wondering why I would do that."

Instead of confirming, he asked, "How do you feel about Burke?"

"He's a good guy."

"Romantically," her father added.

"There is no romantically. I just think he's down-to-earth and fun. I like him."

"In spite of the fact that he went along with your scheme the first time you met?"

"We already talked about this," she reminded him.

"Not all of it. I see the looks between you two when you think no one is watching. I know how a man looks when he's got ideas about a woman—"

"Dad." She held up her hand for him to stop. They'd had this awkward conversation when she was about twelve and that was an experience she didn't want to repeat. "I get your drift. Enough said. There's no need to discuss this."

"I disagree. You know I'm concerned. Can't help it." He shrugged. "And I'm not so sure you don't have feelings for the guy."

"I told you—"

This time he held up a hand to stop her. "You're acting as if I'm going to chase him off. That's not the case."

She looked at him, eyes narrowing suspiciously. "Then what are you trying to say?"

"If you like him, I'm okay with that."

She wasn't. "Seriously, Dad, I'm not stupid or desperate enough to fall for a guy who isn't staying. And I'm not willing to move to be with him. Blackwater Lake is my home and I love working with you. So, it's settled."

"Look, honey, I know you got pretty banged-up when Violet and Charlie messed you over. Doesn't matter whether or not they meant for it to happen, it still hurt. And Loretta has told me how deeply a teenage girl can feel the pain and hold on to it."

"Loretta said that?"

"She did. A very wise woman." There was a tender expression on his face. "Not that we were talking about you, or anything."

"Of course not," she said drily. But it made her feel a little sad that he'd never had the perspective of a close relationship with a woman when she'd been growing up. "Speaking of Loretta, no offense, but why are you home?"

He shrugged and crossed the space between them, then slung his arm across her shoulders. "I guess I wanted to spend some time with my girl."

"That's nice." She rested her head on his chest for a moment. "Don't worry about me, Dad. I'm fine. Really."

"Of course you are." He sighed. "I guess I just wanted to say that I'm not the best example of getting back on the horse after falling off. And I know that it's hard to do when you've been kicked in the teeth. That sort of thing can shape your life choices."

"Listen to you being all in touch with your feelings."

"This is hard enough without you being a smart aleck." There was a teasing note in his voice. "But seriously, Sydney Marie, do as I say, not as I did. Take a chance. Don't hide from it all."

"Okay, Dad."

But that was easier said than done. She'd been keeping herself isolated for a lot of years and wasn't sure that habit could be broken.

Or that she even wanted to.

Chapter Eleven

"Dad, why can't I go over to Syd's? She said I could go anytime I wanted to run around outside and play ball." Liam's voice had the beginning of a whine.

Burke had just picked him up from school and they were headed back to the office.

"There are a lot of reasons. First, Syd is working and there's no one at the house to supervise you. Don't even say it." He knew what was going through the kid's mind. "I can't stay with you. There's work back at the office. And a surprise for you."

"Me? What is it?" Just like that the whine vanished without a trace.

"If I told you, it wouldn't be a surprise, would it?"

Burke hadn't said anything about family coming to town. Sloan was here with preliminary drawings for the resort. But Burke's father, who had retired from the company, had announced he was coming along, too. In Burke's experience, the man had a way of not showing up and he'd decided not to say anything to Liam and risk disappointing him. If Walker Holden showed up it *would* be a surprise—for Burke, too. But Sloan had texted that the two of them were driving from the airport and given their estimated time of arrival. That would put them at the office when he got there with Liam.

He could hardly blame the boy for wanting to go to Sydney's house. For Burke, though, it wasn't about the house as much as seeing her in it. Or anywhere else for that matter. She was sunshine and flowers. Just looking at her made him feel good. He'd been to some of the fanciest, most expensive restaurants in the world, but hamburgers and wine on her patio had been one of the best meals he'd ever had.

She was a natural with kids, too. Liam really liked her. It was something they both agreed on and that hadn't happened in a long time.

Burke pulled in to the parking lot of the O'Keefe Technology building. Liam jumped out of the car practically before the engine was shut off. After hitting the lock button, Burke hurried after the boy and caught up with him at the lobby elevator. He checked his phone and read Sloan's text. His cousin and father were waiting in Burke's office.

He and Liam rode up together and when the doors opened, the kid was out like a shot, but this time he didn't take off.

"What's the surprise?" he asked. "A new video game? A dog?"

Lydia, his executive assistant, looked up when she heard the boy's voice. "Hey, Liam. How was school?"

"Hi. Okay. What's my surprise?" He marched up to her desk.

"I'm not at liberty to say." Her eyes twinkled when she looked at Burke. "But your afternoon appointment is here."

"Okay. Let's go, son." He put his hand on the boy's shoulder.

"It's just going to be a boring meeting. Do I hafta stay?"

"I'm afraid so. But I'll try to make it quick."

He opened his office door and two men occupied the sofa, coffee in front of them on the table. It took a couple of seconds, then Liam dropped his backpack and raced over.

"Uncle Sloan!" Liam knew the man wasn't an uncle, but Cousin Sloan sounded dumb. When the boy was little they'd settled on the title as a gesture of respect.

"Hey, kid." His cousin grabbed the boy in a bear hug. With Sloan's dark hair and eyes he didn't much look like Burke except for height and body type.

Liam wiggled free and looked at the other man. "Grand-dad!"

"Hello, Liam." Walker Holden embraced his grandson with what looked like genuine affection.

Burke couldn't tell. He didn't recall being on the receiving end of warmth from his father. "Hello, Dad. You're looking well."

The man was about his height and they had the same blue eyes. His father's brown hair was shot with silver. "Burke. It's good to see you."

He shook the offered hand and made sure his grip was firm enough and eye contact held just the right amount of time. Then he met his cousin's gaze and grinned.

"Sloan." Burke grabbed him in a quick hug.

"Is this my surprise?" Liam asked.

"Yes. Uncle Sloan is here on business." He didn't know why his father was there.

"Cool."

"When I told him there was a surprise waiting for him, he was hoping for a video game or a puppy." Burke felt a dash of guilt for not addressing his father's presence, but he didn't know why he'd tagged along.

"A dog sounds like a great idea," Sloan said. "After the meeting we should go to the pet store. This town has one, right?"

Burke shook his head. "I don't know. And it doesn't matter. There's no way we're getting a dog. We're stuck at the lodge for the duration and that's no place for a dog."

"I bet Sydney would keep a dog for me and I could go visit." Liam looked up hopefully.

"That's not something I would even ask her to do." That, Burke thought, was how good she was with kids. Obviously his son trusted her completely.

"Who's Sydney?" Walker asked. "A local contractor?"

"She's awesome," Liam said. "She and her dad have a garage. She let me watch while she did a tune-up. And I got to hand her tools."

"So, Sydney is a she?" Sloan got that expression on his face, as if to say there was something going on.

"Sydney McKnight. She's a friend," Burke explained. "I did her a favor and she returned it. Her uncle runs the county permit office. She told him I'm a nice guy."

"Clearly her judgment is impaired," Sloan joked.

"And you like her?" Walker put a hand on his grandson's shoulder.

"She's cool. So is her dad. She cooked hamburgers for me and Dad the other night. Then she let me play with her brother's old soccer ball. It was fun."

"So, you like it here in Blackwater Lake?" The older man looked as if it really mattered that the boy was happy.

Liam thought for a moment. "I miss Chicago and my house. And Mary. But I have a friend at school now. Todd. His mom is a friend of Syd's."

And her friend's husband was Syd's old boyfriend. Yet somehow she'd found a way to forgive Violet for the past. It still amazed him. "My son is the only kid in his class who lives in a hotel."

"Yeah. That part stinks."

Burke explained that single-family living space was scarce in this town. And rentals were practically nonexistent. The lodge was the best place for visitors to stay. When notified about his cousin's trip with his father, he'd booked rooms right away and fortunately there were vacancies.

"I knew this area was crying for more housing," Sloan declared. "And I'm anxious to show you the preliminary sketches. They're on your desk."

"The architect is an award-winning designer and someone I've worked with before," Walker said. "I'm pleased with what he's done."

Burke held back the urge to say he'd try not to hold that against the man. "Liam, do you have homework?"

"Some math. And reading."

"Why don't you go in the other room with Lydia. It will be quieter there."

"But, I want to hang out with Granddad and Uncle Sloan."

"That's funny." Burke looked down at the boy. "A little while ago you didn't want to be here for a boring meeting."

"That's before I knew it was with them." He looked at the two and grinned when Sloan winked.

"You'll see them later. Get your homework done and we'll do something fun after." They stared at each other for several moments in what was becoming a standoff. Finally Burke said, "This is not negotiable. The sooner you get at it, the sooner you can visit."

"Your father is right, Liam," Walker said.

Burke was surprised his father had backed him up. The feeling of having the man in his corner was weird and suspicious.

"Okay." The single word came out of his son's mouth along with a big sigh.

"This won't take long, kid," Sloan said. "Then I'll spring you."

"Thanks, Uncle Sloan. 'Bye, Granddad."

After Liam had left the office Burke asked, "Why are you here, Dad?"

Some emotion flitted through the man's blue eyes. Defensiveness? Guilt? Sadness? It wasn't clear and then the expression was gone. "I wanted to see how Liam was doing. And you."

Now it was really weird. After his mother died, the man was gone all the time. He'd never shown up much at all, let alone to see how Burke was doing.

"We're fine." *Wary, skeptical, but otherwise all right,* he thought. "I'm really anxious to see the sketches."

"Let's do it." Sloan walked over to the desk and picked up the tube lying on top of it. He opened up one end and shook out the sheaf of papers rolled up inside, then spread them out.

Burke carefully inspected each sketch. There was a condo complex with parking nestled in the mountains near the ski area. A retail multi-use compound with living space above. Restaurants and bars. And all of it was just wrong. It was glass and chrome, modern, cold and impersonal.

He looked at his cousin. "This is an awful monstrosity."

Sloan's eyes narrowed. "Don't sugarcoat it. Tell us how you really feel."

"I'm sorry. But all this glass—"

"To showcase the spectacular views of the lake and mountains," his cousin explained.

"I get that. But there are ways to do it so that a building doesn't look like it was lifted from the skyline of Chicago or New York and plopped down in Montana."

"I disagree, Burke." Walker was flipping through the drawings. "When there's snow on the slopes, these structures will blend in."

"With the ice maybe." Burke shook his head. "What about the trees? Or when it's spring and the ice has melted?"

"I agree with Uncle Walker. I like where the architect is going with this concept."

"That's because you live in the city. But what about when you want to get away from it all? If you were from around here, you'd see where *I'm* going with this. The mayor needs to see and approve of these. And she won't. Because the town is going to hate them."

"Really? The town?" There was sarcasm in Sloan's voice. "I'm sort of surprised you're thinking in terms of what the town will think."

"That's because you haven't spent time here in Blackwater Lake. This is one of those rare places that takes on a character of its own and that's a reflection of the people here. They're supportive, warm and welcoming." He pointed to the drawing of the glass-and-metal structure. "Not icy and aloof. The town will hate that," he said again.

"The town may just have to live with it."

Syd was part of the town and wouldn't like living with it.

"We need new sketches and a different focus from someone who knows and understands the area." Burke looked from one man to the other. "Syd's sister-in-law lives locally and is an architect. She used to work for Hart Industries in Dallas."

"I've heard of them," Sloan said. "Impressive body of work."

"Let's give Ellie a chance to come up with something. If the mayor agrees with me. In the meantime, I'll show you around so you can get a feel for what I'm talking about."

Sloan and his father exchanged glances, then both nodded.

Burke was glad they were open-minded. That was easier than trying to explain the unexplainable. Which was that it wasn't the town's feelings he cared about. Good, bad or indifferent, Sydney McKnight was the one he wanted to please.

Sydney sat beside Burke and across the table from Liam at the Grizzly Bear Diner. She wasn't sure how this seating arrangement happened; she would have been better off looking at the two Holden men, but Liam sat first. Then she'd slid in on the other side of the booth and Burke joined her. Now their thighs and arms were touching and she expected to spontaneously combust any second.

"So when did your father leave town?" she asked, trying to take her mind off what was happening to her body.

"This morning."

She'd met his father and cousin at dinner. Burke had called to invite her and warned that his family would be there. She'd been a little nervous. The reaction meant that she cared what Walker and Sloan Holden thought of her, a clear indication that she wasn't indifferent to Burke. But dinner had gone well as far as she could tell.

And tonight at the diner had been fun. As Burke had once predicted, Liam loved the place.

She took the last bite of her salad, chewed and swallowed. "I like your father."

"Really?" Burke looked skeptical.

"He's very charming." Meeting Walker had been like looking into the future and seeing how his son would look when he was in his sixties. Still outrageously handsome and incredibly distinguished. "You look a lot like him."

"No, I don't."

"Dad, people say that all the time. And that I look like you. Which means I look like Granddad."

Unlike his father, the younger Holden seemed to have a

close relationship with Walker. Syd saw the resemblance between all three.

"Your granddad is a very handsome man. There are a lot worse things than looking like him. And without extensive plastic surgery, there's not much you can do but embrace it and move on."

"Okay. Consider this moving on." Burke set his used paper napkin on the empty plate in front of him. "If we're all finished here, I suggest we go down the street to Potter's Ice Cream Parlor for dessert."

"That's a great idea, Dad."

Syd smiled at the boy. He was so different from the hostile, unhappy child he'd been just a couple weeks ago after being dragged to Blackwater Lake. Making a friend had helped but couldn't completely explain the transformation. Burke must be doing a lot right, though she suspected he wouldn't see it.

"Earth to Syd—"

"Hmm?" She blinked and looked up at him. "What?"

"How do you feel about ice cream?"

"In twenty-five words or less I have a deep and personal bond with it that is both celebratory and therapeutic."

"Huh?" Liam looked at her as if she was speaking in an obscure foreign dialect.

"I think that means she likes it when she's happy and uses it as a coping mechanism when she's sad."

"Very intuitive of you, Mr. Holden," she mused.

"Does that mean we can get some?" Liam demanded.

She and Burke grinned at each other and said, "Yes."

"Okay, I'm finished," the boy said. He crammed the last chicken tender in his mouth and mumbled, "What are we waiting for?"

"The check," Syd reminded him.

"Oh, right."

Burke signaled the server, who brought the bill over, along with a plastic grizzly bear toy and a T-shirt for Liam.

Syd was glad they were finally getting ready to vacate the small booth. She'd been in this place a bazillion times and sat everywhere, always with plenty of room. This was her second time sitting beside Burke with legs, thighs and arms brushing, and her reaction was the same. She was hot all over and ice cream would help cool her off.

Besides, she liked hanging out with Liam and his father. They were friends, but she would breathe easier if she could be his friend with a generous buffer zone around them when hanging out.

After paying the check at the register, they walked outside—Liam first while Burke held the door for her. That was nice. A gentleman as always. Burke clearly didn't like being compared to his father, but Walker was a courtly man and it was likely his son had picked up the trait from him.

They headed down the street past Tonya's Treasures, the town souvenir-and-gift shop. Beyond it was the ice cream parlor and The Harvest Café, which shared a connecting door and were now both Maggie's businesses. The latter had once been a dry cleaning store, but the owners had let the lease run out. They retired and moved to California to be near their grandkids. Maggie Potter and her partner, Lucy Bishop, seemed to have the business under control.

When they reached Maggie's, Burke opened the door and Liam started to go in. He put his hand on the boy's shoulder to stop him and said, "Ladies first, pal."

Syd's heart actually fluttered as she passed without actually brushing up against him. So much for her buffer-zone theory. "Thanks."

"My pleasure." His voice went husky on the last word, giving a hint to his thoughts.

The interior of the ice cream parlor was cheerful and

bright. Pictures on the walls were of ice-cream scoops, sundaes, shakes and cakes. Some with sprinkles, others with whipped cream and a cherry. There were small, round tables filling the center of the room and metal chairs with heart-shaped backs and red padded seats.

Syd walked over to the glass display case, surprised to see Maggie behind it. Her friend had an office upstairs over the café, where she worked keeping the books and ordering supplies. Manning The Harvest Café counter was handled by her partner, and normally a part-time high-school kid was here in the evening on the ice cream side. But not tonight.

"Hi, Maggie. What are you doing here?"

"Taylor broke her wrist at cheerleading practice. It's kind of important to be able to use it when scooping ice cream. Couldn't find anyone to fill in on such short notice. Most important—she'll be fine."

"Where's Danielle?"

"She's with my tenant, Josie."

Syd remembered her friend explaining about renting out one of her upstairs bedrooms to her friend for the extra income. Another bonus, apparently, was child care for emergency situations like this.

"Hi, Maggie. This is my son, Liam." Burke came up behind Syd. She could feel the heat from his body and shivered at the closeness.

"Hi." Maggie bent down and looked through the glass because she couldn't see over it. "Nice to meet you."

The boy waved in response. "Do you get all the ice cream you can eat?"

"Liam," Burke said, "that's not an appropriate question."

"It's okay." Maggie laughed. "If he asked how much I weigh or my age, that would be inappropriate. And the answer is yes, I own the place and can eat as much as I want. But you'd be surprised how fast you get tired of ice cream."

"No way." Father and son spoke together and with great feeling.

Syd laughed and wondered if Burke realized how alike the two of them were, how much they had in common. The father had come a long way since the boy had come to live with him.

"What can I get you?" Maggie asked.

It was obvious that Liam knew exactly what he wanted because he immediately ordered a scoop of cookies-and-cream, and another of chocolate caramel with whipped cream, nuts and a cherry.

"A man who knows his own mind. Coming right up." Maggie put it together and handed over the cup at the low counter by the cash register.

"Thanks," the boy said politely, then took his dessert to a table to start eating before it melted.

"Syd? The usual?" Maggie asked.

"Of course."

Burke arched one eyebrow. "One of the many small-town-living perks is that your ice-cream preference is not a secret. But if you got wild with a scoop of peanut butter and bubble gum, people would talk."

"It's true." She took the waffle cone with vanilla ice cream that Maggie handed her and tasted it. "So good."

When Burke ordered two scoops of rocky road, Syd wondered if there was any deeper psychological meaning in the choice. Then he made sure Maggie knew he wanted it "neat."

She pulled a cup from the stack on the counter. "I'm guessing that means no topping or embellishment of any kind?"

"I'm a simple man."

Syd could have argued that point until hell wouldn't

have it, but decided to keep the thoughts to herself. Again Burke paid and they sat with Liam at a table in the center of the room to eat.

The bell over the door rang and in came her father and Loretta Goodson, hand in hand. They were smiling at each other, clearly in love, and Syd felt a rush of conflicting emotion. She was happy for them, of course, but there was a darker feeling, too, something very close to envy. She felt like a selfish toad.

"Hey," Liam said when he saw who it was. "Over here."

The newcomers tore their gazes from each other and glanced at the table. Tom waved. "Great minds think alike. Can we join you?"

"We'll make room." Liam jumped up and pulled over two chairs from another table.

Burke slid closer to Syd, closer than he'd been at the diner. It was cozy. She'd be lying if she said it wasn't nice. And it was the death blow to her fantasy that a buffer zone would make her attraction to the man harmless.

In a few minutes the older couple sat in the chairs between Burke and Liam.

"Madam Mayor, I don't think you've met my son. Liam, this is Mayor Goodson."

"It's great to meet you." The mayor started to shake his hand, then laughed. "Mine are sticky."

"Me, too." Liam grinned.

"It's becoming a family affair," Loretta said. "It was nice to meet your father and cousin. I hope they feel it was worth the trip here. The unscheduled visit saved a lot of time."

"How so?" Syd asked.

"The resort's overall concept in their rough draft was unacceptable, and the town council agrees." The mayor took a bite of ice cream, then swallowed. "You were right, Burke. The buildings were modern and sleek, which would be fine somewhere else. But we were looking for quaint and charming. Sort of sophisticated mountain getaway."

Burke nodded. "You can thank Syd."

"Me?" She nearly choked on her waffle cone. "What did I do?"

"You tutored me in what's best for Blackwater Lake."

"We never discussed architectural design," she protested.

"True," he agreed. "But you told me what the town stands for and the values of folks who live here. I just knew sleek and modern wasn't it."

"I'm surprised you're that perceptive," Syd commented. "No offense."

"None taken. And, for the record, I'm usually not that astute. But your commitment to this community is inspiring."

"That's my girl." Her father looked proud.

"I'm going to work with Ellie on a new concept. We'll get it right."

Loretta nodded her approval. "Ellie's good. But you have to know we'll keep an eye on everything."

"I'd expect nothing less," he said. "But you can trust me not to mess it up."

Syd wasn't so sure the same could be said of her and she didn't mean building a mountain resort. The misgivings were all about herself. His admission about being perceptive with her had come out of the blue and she didn't want to believe it. If she did, going all in with her heart was a real possibility.

Earlier she'd noticed that he'd come a long way from the stressed-out father who'd been forced by circumstances to bring his son here. But that was no guarantee he'd changed his mind about a family. Or any other commitment.

If she let in the notion of him being different with her,

that opened up a very real possibility of her getting hurt. Something that never occurred to her when she'd started this whole thing.

Chapter Twelve

Sydney walked into the Fireside Restaurant at Blackwater Lake Lodge and Burke thought she was the most beautiful woman he'd ever seen. It wasn't boasting to say that a man in his position had been around some of the most stunning women on the planet, but none of them could hold a candle to Sydney McKnight. Her long dark hair gleamed even in subdued restaurant lighting and fell past her shoulders like silk.

No little black dress tonight—it was sexy black slacks instead. Her top was sheer chiffon with a camisole underneath. Four-inch platform heels made her legs look a mile long, but mostly he couldn't shake the image of them wrapped around his waist.

That thought made him ache with need.

He'd been wanting to have her to himself ever since that night he'd taken her home and nearly ended up in her bed. With Liam here there hadn't been an opportunity for a second chance, but tonight was the night. Hopefully.

There had been a look in her dark eyes that he'd swear was a longing that matched his own and that wasn't ego talking, either, just experience.

When the restaurant hostess pointed out the table where he waited, Syd gave him a big smile, then shook her head at something the woman said before walking over to him.

Burke stood to greet her. He fully intended to give her a friendly peck on the cheek, but somehow his lips found their way to hers. And breaking off the contact took more willpower than he would have imagined.

"Hi." He took her hands in his own and squeezed.

"Hi." She seemed a little winded and it had to be from the kiss. No way could she have run fast enough in those heels to be out of breath.

Burke pulled out the chair at a right angle to his and held it for her to sit. When she was settled, he sat down beside her, wishing they were as close as a few nights ago at the ice cream parlor with her father and the mayor, when their thighs had brushed repeatedly. It was the most intimately he'd been able to touch her for far too long.

"I'm glad you were free for dinner," he said.

"Boy, were you lucky I wasn't tied up," she teased. "My social calendar is just packed. I couldn't get another engagement in if I used a shoehorn."

"Very funny." He signaled the waiter to bring over two glasses and the bottle of wine he'd already ordered. "I bare my soul and look what happens."

"You called because you were at loose ends with Liam sleeping over at Todd's house." She gave him a wry look. "If there was any soul-baring going on, I missed it. And that's a shame. I would have liked some souvenir pictures."

"You mock me. That hurts," he said, trying to look deeply wounded.

After the bottle was uncorked, the waiter poured a small amount for Burke and waited for his approval before filling Syd's wineglass. "I'll bring bread," he said. "Is there anything else I can get for you right now?"

"Not at the moment," Burke answered. "We'll order in a little while."

When they were alone he held up his glass. "What should we drink to?"

"I don't know. You decide."

He thought for a moment then said, "Here's to my good fortune that you had an opening in your busy social calendar for a lonely bachelor."

She looked sympathetic before nodding her approval. "To that."

"How was your day?" He sipped from his glass, then set it down and looked at her.

"Busy. Folks are getting their cars ready for winter. It's already October and before you know it the cold weather will be here. There are a lot of tune-ups and inquiries about snow tires."

He wondered if the winter was more brutal here than in Chicago. Being more rural than urban would pose different weather-related challenges. "It is getting to be that time of the year."

"Yeah. If I had my way, I'd winter in Tahiti."

"You don't like the cold?" he asked.

"If you polled people, I don't think you'd find many checking the 'love it' box on the questionnaire."

"Do you go somewhere tropical to get a break and thaw out?" He would love to take her to Tahiti. Seeing her in a bikini… Now there was a souvenir picture. Or out of it—even better.

"I keep threatening to go to Hawaii or Florida."

"Why haven't you?"

"I didn't want to leave my dad alone." She shrugged.

"Now you know he has…companionship," he said diplomatically.

She gave him a warning look. "Don't even hint about them sleeping together. I don't ever want that thought in my head because I'll never get it out."

"Didn't one of your brothers stop by his house unexpectedly and find them in a compromising situation—"

"Burke—" There was a warning expression in her eyes and the tone in her voice threatened serious consequences.

He would take his chances. "Your brothers must be proud. His…athleticism…bodes well for them as they get older."

"One more word and I'll put my hands over my ears and start humming." The way her full lips twitched hinted that she wasn't as bothered by this topic of conversation as she pretended.

"Okay, I'll be good."

Tilting her head to the side in a little bit of a flirt, she said, "Not too good."

"Time will tell."

There was a look in her eyes that promised heaven. Dear God, she was going to kill him.

"My point in bringing up your father's…situation…is that you don't have to feel as if he needs someone to look out for him."

"It's a difficult habit to break," she admitted.

"A midwinter trip to Bora-Bora would be a good start. You should go with a friend."

"Getting away isn't easy for most people." She toyed with her wineglass. "And the airport is pretty far. It's a particular challenge in a blizzard."

"Pretty soon there will be an airport closer. And those are just excuses." Burke studied her. "You're lonely, too, aren't you?"

Her gaze snapped to his. "I didn't say that."

"You didn't have to. Takes one to know one."

Without conceding the truth of his out-of-the-box statement, she made one of her own. "So, you're pretty hostile to your father."

And he'd been so careful to keep it from showing. "What gave me away?"

"Pretty much everything." She reached beneath the cloth napkin covering the bread and pulled out a crusty roll, then put it on her small plate. After sliding a pat of butter beside it, she met his gaze. "It was little things. The way your eyes got angry when you looked at him. A tone when you talked. Irritated, I guess, at anything he said, no matter how harmless. And body language—your shoulders tensed. Or you almost winced every time Walker opened his mouth."

He wasn't sure which was worse—that he felt antagonistic toward his father or that she was dead-on about it. "Wow."

"You didn't tell me I'm wrong." She broke a piece off the roll, buttered it and popped the morsel into her mouth.

He could dance around it. He usually did. But for some reason, he wanted her to know he had a good reason for feeling the way he did.

"I guess I never got over the way he acted after my mother died," he admitted. "And he wasn't around a whole lot when she was battling breast cancer."

The teasing challenge in her eyes was chased away by sympathy. She reached over and covered his hand with her own. "I'm sorry, Burke. That must have been so difficult."

"That means a lot coming from you. You never even knew your mother." He turned his hand over and linked his fingers with hers.

"It was different for me because she was never part of my life so I didn't feel the emptiness when she was gone. I guess I envied my friends who had moms, but people here in Blackwater Lake filled in."

"How?"

"Maggie's mom took me for my first bra. If I needed a dress for prom, there was always a woman to help. Dad told me about sex and all that." She grinned. "It was an experience. For us both."

"I bet."

"My point is that you can't miss what you didn't have. But you lost your mother at such a vulnerable age." Empathy shimmered in her eyes.

"Yeah." It had been the loneliest time in his life. "My father went right back to work. He was always busy, but after the funeral it was like busy on steroids."

"And you're angry about that."

"Let me count the ways." He tried to smile but it didn't happen. "He never showed up for anything going on in my life. Holidays were hit-and-miss. It was like losing both parents at the same time."

"Oh, Burke—" She sighed and squeezed his hand. "I was too little to remember how dad was after losing my mother. But people who were there say he buried himself in work because he couldn't deal with the grief, but everyone knew he loved her very much. Plus he had to make a living with three mouths to feed. Maybe men handle loss by burying their feelings in something familiar and not talking about it."

"Maybe."

But Burke wasn't ready to let go of the resentment. It hit him again when his own son was born and he had no role model to draw from. Mostly he tried to do the opposite of what his father had done, but somehow he'd fallen into the workaholic pattern.

"I couldn't help noticing that Liam is genuinely fond of his grandfather. And vice versa. There must be a reason. Kids aren't easily fooled." She thought for a moment.

"And here's a radical thought. It might help to talk about your feelings with Walker."

"Maybe," he said again.

But he was thinking hell would freeze over before that happened. And the attitude must have shown in his voice and body language because Syd nodded but didn't say more about that.

"I also noticed that Liam seems to be settling in nicely."

"He's...adjusting." He appreciated the topic change and suspected she'd purposely steered the conversation in a more positive direction. "Better than I thought he would."

"Has it occurred to you that settling in wouldn't have gone so well if you're as bad a father as you seem to think?"

"No, it never did. I think any credit goes to you, your dad and the school."

She shook her head in faux frustration. "For an intelligent man you're not so smart about some stuff."

"Like what?"

"You're a single dad and Liam is a great kid. Work is demanding so others have to fill in, but he spends more time with you than anyone. Something positive you're doing must be rubbing off on him."

Burke wasn't completely convinced, but admitted, if only to himself, that there could be some truth in what she said.

"Are you hungry?" he asked.

"Starved."

He signaled the waiter to bring menus. "Then we should order."

"Sounds good to me."

He planned to do as many courses as possible to keep her here. Saying goodbye after dinner with her always seemed to come too soon and he was never ready. Idly he wondered if that feeling would ever go away.

Syd was having a wonderful time and it felt as if they'd occupied the intimate corner table for two at Fireside for minutes instead of hours. Wine, salad, entrées, dessert and after-dinner drinks had been consumed and Burke was signing the check.

But she wasn't ready for the evening to end.

He put the pen inside the leather holder with the bill, then looked at her. "Are you ready to go?"

"Yes," she lied.

They stood and he waited for her to precede him to the exit. On the way he said good-night to the waiter, server, busboy and hostess, calling each one by their given name. Obviously he'd gotten to know them, but she supposed that happened when one lived in a hotel.

He settled his hand at the small of her back and the contact touched off a chain reaction of nerve endings that sensitized every inch of her skin. She wanted to snuggle in closer but resisted. There was nothing more awkward than being obvious about wanting someone and getting the message that they didn't share your feelings. Burke would have to make the first move.

Just before stepping from the privacy of the long hallway into the lodge's lobby, Burke stopped and looked down. "I had a really good time tonight."

"Me, too."

"Tomorrow is Saturday."

"You're kidding." She pretended shock and surprise. "Really? I had no idea."

"Let me rephrase." He looked down for a moment, then met her gaze. "I don't have to work. Do you?"

"I do, as a matter of fact. Saturday is busy at the garage." Syd's heart beat a little faster as she had a hunch where he was going with this.

"Oh. Then you don't want to be out too late."

"A girl has to get her beauty rest," she agreed.

He put his palm flat on the wall beside her and moved closer, trapping her in the best possible way against his body. "If you were any more beautiful, that face would have to be registered as a lethal weapon with the sheriff's office."

Her heart started to beat even faster as his look went from lazy to lusty in a nanosecond. "So…" She swallowed once. "Wild guess here…you don't want to say good-night yet?"

"You're very perceptive." He gently brushed the hair from her cheek, then traced his index finger along her jaw.

"We should take a walk." She glanced down at her feet. "Although I don't know how far I'd get in these shoes."

"That depends on where you want to go." His voice was a ragged whisper.

Her heart skipped a beat, then kicked in again, hammering harder than ever. "I'd crawl on my hands and knees if necessary. Depending on the destination."

The corners of his mouth curved up as his gaze danced over her face. Then he lowered his head and kissed her. His lips were soft, warm, coaxing and caressing. Pressing his body even closer to hers, he let her know he wanted her.

Tracing her lips with his tongue, he teased her mouth open then slipped inside. He tasted good, she thought, like wine and the chocolate cake they'd just shared. She didn't consciously put her arms around his shoulders, but she suddenly realized they were there. In the blink of an eye she was incredibly turned on and it was a miracle she could think rationally enough to make a point.

Against his mouth she whispered, "Someone is going

to walk by and they might not say it out loud, but you can bet they'll be thinking we should get a room."

His smile was wicked. "As luck would have it, I already have one."

"That is lucky."

He moved back a step, then grabbed her hand. "I don't think we want to go through the lobby. Let's take the back way."

She was trapped in a sensuous haze and let him lead her to an elevator in a more discreet location. He pushed the up button and almost immediately the doors opened. They got in and rode to the top floor of the lodge, where he pointed to the end of the hall and the double-door entry of his suite. It seemed far away, too far, but with him holding tightly to her hand, she matched her steps to his long stride. After inserting his key card, he opened the door and let her go inside first.

Behind her there was the sound of a click and then the entryway's overhead light went on. In front of her was a sitting area with a couch, chairs and tables. A flat-screen TV was mounted on the wall. On the far side of the room was a formal cherrywood dining table and six chairs.

She turned to look up at Burke. "I've never been in a suite before."

"What do you think?"

"Rich people really are different."

"Not that much." He took her hand and they walked to the right, stopping at the double doors.

He opened one to reveal a king-size bed, sitting area with a plush love seat and French doors leading to a balcony that overlooked the mountains. The only light was drifting in from the other room and that made erotic shadows in this one.

"Be it ever so humble…" He took off his suit jacket and tossed it on the tufted, cream-colored bench at the foot of the bed. Then he loosened his silk tie, undid the button at his neck and slid it from under the starched collar of his white dress shirt.

Burke removed her small evening bag from her fingers and gently put it by his coat. Then he looked down at her and said, "Where were we?"

She stepped out of her heels and felt even shorter than usual when looking up at him. "I think this is where we left off."

Moving closer, she started undoing the buttons down the front of his shirt before tugging it from the waistband of his slacks. After spreading wide the sides, she rested her palms on the muscular contours of his chest. The dusting of hair tickled her fingers as she slid them down, exploring the feel of him to her heart's content.

When she reached his rib cage, just above his belt, she must have hit a very sensitive spot judging by his sharp intake of breath.

Burke caught her wrist in a strong yet gentle grip. His breathing was harsh and uneven. "My turn."

There were no buttons on her top, so he gripped the chiffon and camisole together and pulled them up and off as she lifted her arms to assist.

His gaze caught fire when he saw her black bra and he shook his head regretfully. "As much as I like the way you look, that has to come off."

Without a word, she turned her back and let him undo the clasp. His hands settled on her shoulders and brushed the satin straps down until the wispy garment fell at her feet. He circled an arm around her and nestled her back against his front then used both hands to cup her bare breasts.

He kissed his way down her neck and with thumb and forefinger toyed with her nipples. She tried to hold it in, but a moan slipped past her lips as the exquisite torture went on and on until she was sure she wouldn't be able to stand it. While she was occupied by the intense pleasure of his touch, he reached down to her waistband to undo the button and lower the zipper of her slacks. The silky material slid easily down her legs and she stepped out of them.

He splayed one big hand over her middle and slid the other down between her legs, cupping her there. His ragged breathing stirred the hair by her ear and his voice was even more ragged as he whispered to her what he wanted, what he yearned to do with her.

The next thing she knew he'd yanked down the bed's comforter and blanket and bared the sheets beneath. He scooped her up into his arms then settled her in the center of the big mattress. Not taking his eyes off her, he set a world record removing his clothes. The expression in his eyes turned dark and intense as she shimmied out of her black panties. Then he slid into bed beside her, reaching out and pulling her against his warm, bare skin.

He brushed his wide palm over the indentation of her waist, over the swell of her hip, then flattened on her abdomen. This time when he caressed between her legs there was no wisp of lace blocking the touch. He rubbed a thumb over the bundle of feminine nerve endings and she believed it a very real possibility that she could go up in flames.

Before she could tell him what she wanted, what she'd craved for so long, he reached into the nightstand and pulled something out. Through a lovely daze, she realized that he'd opened a condom and put it on. Then he gently eased her to her back, braced his forearms on either side of her to take most of his weight and slowly entered her.

Feminine muscles wrapped around him and nerve endings wept at the glorious intrusion. She pulled her heels up higher on the bed, making the contact even more exquisite. Moments later, pleasure blasted through her in a nearly spontaneous explosion.

Burke pushed into her one more time, then went still and groaned, finding his own release. For a long, lovely moment they just held on to each other as shock waves turned to ripples and their breathing slowed to something resembling normal. Truthfully, the meaning of normal had forever changed for her.

He rested his forehead to hers. "That was…"

"Nice," she said.

He lifted his head and even in the dim light his wry expression was visible. "You couldn't think of a more enthusiastic adjective than *nice?*"

"Awesome? Amazing? Spectacular? Great." She shrugged and the hair on his chest rubbed her breasts, sending tingles up and down her spine. "They're all clichés."

"What we just did rates a better description than *nice,*" he said.

Sex with Burke Holden was so awesome and amazing that she would swear it rocked her soul. And that was a scary thought. She figured he wouldn't appreciate knowing that and she didn't want to make herself that vulnerable by saying it out loud.

"Yes, it was better than nice," she agreed.

"Are you okay, Syd?"

"Of course." But she didn't lift her gaze any higher than his collarbone.

"I'll be right back." He rolled away and the bed dipped and rose as he left it. "Don't move."

Her body felt boneless and she couldn't move if she'd wanted to. Syd put her forearm over her eyes, but still sensed when a light went on nearby and heard running water. How she wished that she was better at hiding her feelings. She had wanted this almost from the first time she'd seen him drive into McKnight Automotive.

And now she couldn't shake the sensation that it had been a mistake because it had been so awesome, amazing, spectacular and great. But the last thing she wanted was to be that type of woman, the one who wanted it until she got it and then played hurt.

Why couldn't a girl know she was going to have second thoughts before jumping into the deep end of the pool?

The light went off and seconds later Burke was back, pulling her into his arms. "Okay. Talk to me. What's going on in that mind of yours? And please don't say you're fine, because I know you're not."

It took several moments for her to figure out what she wanted to say and he let her take the time.

"I guess I want you to know that casual sex isn't what I do. One-night stands aren't my thing."

He nodded his understanding. "And if I thought it was your thing, I wouldn't be here."

She rested her cheek on his chest and settled her arm over his flat belly. "You wouldn't?"

"No." He kissed the top of her head. "I like you, Syd. A lot."

"I feel the same about you." Maybe more than like.

"And that's why I want to be completely honest with you."

"Oh?" This was where he said what she'd been thinking, that it was a mistake they shouldn't make again. She braced herself.

"I want you again."

"You do?" She wished it was possible to see his face, but he'd rested his chin on the top of her head.

"Yes. And I hope you want me. This isn't casual for me, but I also can't make any promises."

"I don't expect any." She knew how he felt about commitment. He'd been completely up front about that.

He raised up on an elbow and looked down, studying her. "Can we take this one day at a time? That's the smart play."

"It is," she agreed.

God help her. She was far gone enough to take whatever he could give, but there was a part of her that longed for a promise of forever.

Chapter Thirteen

"This is fun, Dad."

Liam kicked the soccer ball somewhere in Burke's general direction and he jogged over to get it. They were in Sydney's backyard on a beautiful Sunday afternoon while she was inside cooking dinner for them.

"It is fun." Not in the same league as what he and Syd had done in his bed the other night. But it really wasn't fair to compare the two. Bonding with his son was a blessing he honestly had never expected to have. Physically bonding with Syd had been mind-blowing.

If he was being honest it was more than physical. There was a connection and it was more than he'd anticipated. He liked women; he dated. And he walked away. But there was something about Syd that he couldn't put into words, qualities that drew him. Things that had nothing to do with what she looked like. Not a single woman he'd dated had come close to the wonder that was Sydney McKnight.

It had bothered him a little when she didn't push back

on his declaration that he couldn't make any promises. But then, she'd once expected promises from a guy and he'd made them to someone else. Still, that was a long time ago and he wondered what she wanted now.

Liam stood across the yard, hands on hips. "Hey, Dad. You gonna kick the ball or stand there and think about it?"

It was an interesting experience hearing your own words coming out of your child's mouth. He hadn't even been thinking about kicking the ball. Images of Syd in black bra and panties? Yes. Kicking the ball? No. His concentration was messed up because pretty much what he wanted to focus on was her. But that wasn't fair to his son.

"Okay, kid. Comin' at you. Get ready. Think you can handle it?"

The boy grinned. "No problem."

Burke kicked it pretty hard and Liam concentrated, judging the path, moving a little to his right. He stopped the ball with his foot, nudged it to the side, then sent it back.

"You're getting pretty good, son."

"Thanks. I've been practicing with Todd. He said maybe I could join his soccer team. The season's already started, but there might be an opening. Do you think that would be okay? I know we have to go back to Chicago, but I was thinking maybe in the meantime?"

The kid was making a thorough case for it as if he expected to be turned down. "I don't see why not. I'll get the information from Todd's parents and check in to it. Let's see if we can make that happen."

"Cool."

The ball came to him and Burke stopped it with his foot, then picked it up. "We should probably have something to drink. Syd went to all the trouble to make lemonade and leave it out here for us."

"I am kind of thirsty." Liam ran across the yard to the patio table holding a pitcher and two glasses.

"Here you go." Burke held out a full glass after pouring the sweet, cold liquid into it.

"Thanks, Dad."

They sat down side by side in the padded chairs and guzzled lemonade.

"This is pretty good stuff." He watched his son drag his forearm across his mouth to blot the excess liquid. Then the boy seemed to realize what he'd done and glanced up, waiting to hear what he'd done wrong.

Normally Burke would have called him on the breach of good manners, but two things stopped him. Number one: they were alone and this was a guy moment. No ladies present to be offended. And, number two: he didn't want to spoil this father-son moment with a lecture that usually ended by saying Liam wasn't being raised by wolves. There were teachable situations, but this wasn't one of them.

Syd was the one who'd made him see that you picked your battles. It was a parent's responsibility to make sure his child knew what was and wasn't acceptable in polite society. But the chances were pretty good that someday when he took a girl out for dinner Liam wouldn't use his sleeve for a napkin. Or he would only do it once and get an advanced degree from the school of hard knocks.

"Dad?"

"What, son?"

"I'm sorry I was such a dork when I first got here."

Burke couldn't have been more surprised if an alien ship landed in the yard and an extraterrestrial said "take me to your leader." Finally he was able to say, "Don't worry about it. I understand. It was hard for you, leaving your friends and everything that's familiar."

"Yeah." The boy looked down frowning, as if remembering the experience.

"I'm sorry you had to go through that. The good news is that Mary will be okay after rest and recuperation. She's retiring, but we'll figure things out. At least you'll have your house, yard and friends back."

"Yeah," he said again, a little uncertain. "And I'll have to leave the friends I made here. I thought it was boring at first, but I really like Blackwater Lake."

"Good. It's a nice place. And since work will keep me here for a while, I'm glad you like it."

"You know what the best part is?" The boy looked up, a vulnerable expression in his blue eyes.

"What?"

"I get to hang out with you a lot."

"Really?" Burke felt a tightness in his chest. "You like doing stuff together?"

"It's awesome." Liam nodded eagerly. "We don't even have to do stuff. I like just hanging out or watching TV together."

The tightness in his chest squeezed a little more. This was one of those moments that he wished you could hang on the wall and look at when life kicked you in the teeth. But it also pricked his guilt. For a long time he'd been making excuses to justify pushing off his son on the housekeeper, when the truth was that he could adjust other things in order to spend enough time with his child. And he hadn't. It took Blackwater Lake to make him see that things could be different. He could be different.

"I'm sorry, too, Liam."

"What for?"

"I haven't been a very good father to you. I'm always busy. Not around. Blaming it on work."

"Mary says what you do is important. That a lot of people wouldn't have jobs if not for your company."

Even his housekeeper was making excuses for his parenting—or lack thereof. "The truth is that I could have done better as a dad. I love you and I love spending time with you. And I'm making a promise that from now on we'll hang out a lot more."

"Cross your heart?"

Burke made the sign over his heart and held out a closed fist. His son bumped it with his own. This gesture was more sacred than a handshake and again one of those unspoiled moments that stand out in a father's mind.

"You know, Dad, if you don't keep your promise Syd wouldn't like it."

"No, she wouldn't. I've never seen her mad and don't ever want to."

"Me, either," Liam agreed.

They sat there for a few moments and Burke basked in the glow. Everyone he talked to in town said that it would be winter soon, but so far the only sign was that nights were colder. This Indian summer weather fit his mood perfectly, he thought. If he had to give the feeling a name, he would call it contentment. It was noteworthy that he recognized the sensation since it had been in short supply most of his life.

"Dad, when we go back to Chicago, do you think she can come for a visit?"

The words yanked him back but he wasn't sure which "she" his son meant. "Who?"

"Syd. Do you think she could come and see us?" The boy looked up hopefully and his feelings were there for the world to see. He was going to miss her.

"It's all right with me," Burke said. "I hope she'll visit. I'll ask her."

"Then I'm sure she will."

"Why do you think so, son?"

"Anyone can see that she likes you a lot. Do you like her?" Liam asked.

"I would say we're good friends."

Who slept together. But of course he wasn't about to tell that to his eight-year-old son. If Burke was being honest with himself, he would admit that Syd was more than a friend, but how much more?

"Todd is my friend. Do you think I could ask him to visit in Chicago?"

"Of course. But that's up to his parents."

Burke realized that Liam wasn't the only Holden wearing his emotions in plain sight. He'd grown accustomed to seeing Syd almost every day. The frustrations that were constant in his work on a daily basis didn't seem so bad when he knew that night he would spend time with her and talk about it. She was an excellent listener and often had good advice.

Sydney McKnight was a goodbye he wasn't yet prepared to handle.

Hell, the other night after dinner he hadn't been ready to say good-night. That's one reason he'd taken her up to his room. And making love to her was nice.

The word made him smile as he pictured her saying it. Once wasn't enough; he wanted her again. It was another in a growing list of reasons for not wanting to say goodbye to her.

Part of his job involved solving problems. This one was personal and more delicate. But an idea popped into his mind that could fix everything.

Sydney walked from the service bay to the office, where her father was working, and poked her head in. "Hey, Dad. I'm all caught up."

"So you're done for the day?" He looked at his watch and his eyebrows rose. "Before quitting time. Are you that good? Or just motivated to get out of here early because you have a date with Burke?"

"I'm that good," she said with a grin.

There was no date, but a girl could hope. Still, it was Monday and therefore a school night. She completely respected the restrictions that put on Burke's social life.

Alone time with him was precious, but she'd enjoyed hanging out with father and son yesterday. She liked watching the two interact and Liam was just a sweetie. The sullen child she'd first met had disappeared, thanks to whatever Burke was doing.

Syd heard her father's voice and realized she'd been lost in her own thoughts. "I'm sorry. What was that?"

"I said, Loretta and I are going to the diner for dinner. You and Burke and Liam should join us."

"I'm free, but I don't know about the boys."

That's how she'd started thinking about them. The boys. While in the kitchen cooking, she'd glanced out the window and noted identical serious expressions on their faces, indicating a serious discussion underway. Burke had never mentioned what they'd talked about.

But he'd been really attentive afterward. While eating dinner, he'd caressed her thigh underneath the table and stolen kisses when his son was out of the room. There was something different about him, an intensity and focus that were fine-tuned and firing on all cylinders. It was exciting, if a little unsettling. She didn't know what to think. Was he making the most of every moment because the time was fast approaching for him to leave town?

"If I hear from Burke, I'll let you know."

"You could call him," her dad pointed out.

"Guess I'm a little old-fashioned." And maybe a little insecure. A call from him meant he really wanted to see her. "Are you ready to leave?"

"Not yet," he answered. "I'm going to finish ordering

the parts for Floyd Robinson's truck since I have time to kill before meeting Loretta."

"Okay, then. 'Bye, Dad."

"See you, Syd."

She'd just walked outside when her cell rang, making her heart skip. It was like being a teenager again, waiting to hear from that special boy.

She looked at the caller ID and smiled when she recognized that special boy's number. "Hi, there."

"Hey, Syd. It's Burke."

"I knew that."

"Right." His voice was clipped, distracted. "Where are you?"

"Just left the office." She'd just mention dinner. What the heck? He'd called her. "Dad and Loretta are going to the Grizzly Bear Diner. If you and Liam want—"

"There's something I need to talk to you about. Are you going home?" He sounded weird.

"Yes. On my way there now. Why?"

"I'll meet you."

"Burke, what's wrong?" There was no answer and when she looked at the phone it said, *call ended.*

Suddenly her heart wasn't skipping but her stomach was, and not in a happy way. She didn't want to face him in work clothes and needed time to change. It was a challenge to drive as fast as she could and still be just under the speed limit.

After squealing into her driveway, she parked the car, unlocked the door and raced up to her room. She pulled off work pants and shirt then grabbed black jeans and a long-sleeved pink T-shirt. After brushing out her hair, she left it loose around her shoulders, then put on tinted lip gloss.

As she was considering whether or not to put on makeup, the doorbell rang and she scrapped the idea. How she looked wouldn't matter since what he had to say wasn't going to be good. Being a pessimist was a downer but it was better to be realistic and prepared.

She raced downstairs and opened the door. There he was on the porch and the sight of him made her heart swell to the point of aching. His white dress shirt was rumpled and the sleeves were rolled up to mid-forearm. The expensive gray-and-black silk tie was loosened at his throat. Five-o'clock shadow made him look incredibly sexy. If he hadn't said he needed to talk, she would have grabbed that tie and tugged him upstairs.

"Can I come in?"

"Sure." She shook her head to clear it, then stepped back and pulled the door wider.

"Thanks." He walked past her and stopped in the entryway.

"Would you like a beer?"

"Not now." He dragged his fingers through his hair. "There's something I need to talk to you about."

"So you said." She braced herself for the brush-off. "What's up?"

"I think we should get married."

The words started a roaring in her ears, but his expression was intent and sincere. "I'm sorry. We should do what now?"

"Get married."

She felt as if this was some kind of surreal board game and she'd just jumped to the end after skipping major steps in the process.

"What's wrong?" she finally asked.

"Nothing. It's all good." He smiled at her as if that explained everything.

"I think I need just a little more information than that."

"I've been thinking this over all night, but I can see where you'd need context." He met her gaze with a "trust me" expression in his own eyes. "This makes really good sense."

On what planet? she wanted to ask. With an effort she held back and tried not to make a judgment until hearing him out. "Explain it to me."

"You like me—"

"What makes you so sure about that?" Right this minute she wasn't sure how she felt.

"Because you're not the kind of woman who goes to bed with a man unless she has feelings for him. Positive feelings. And believe me I know the difference." His blue eyes darkened with intensity. "And Liam noticed it, too. He said you like me."

"He did?" What was this? Junior high?

"Yes, he did."

She knew she was bad at hiding her feelings but hadn't figured she was so obvious a kid would notice. She wasn't sure why this conversation and his proposal were putting her on the defensive, but his declaration made her want to push back. Except she couldn't deny she really liked him. That was the truth.

"Okay."

"And I like you," he added.

She had to take his word for that because he wasn't as obvious as she was. "Nice of you to say."

"Liam likes you, too. And you're terrific with him."

"He's a great kid."

"See?" He beamed at her as if she was his star pupil. "We could be a family."

That's what she'd always wanted. And her dad wanted it for her. It's what had made her approach Burke in the first place. But this was weird and was probably the reason he'd been acting differently last night.

"A few days ago we agreed to take it one day at a time."

"And today I'm asking you to marry me."

Skeptical and weird was not how she'd expected to feel when a man she cared very much about proposed to her. "What happened to change your mind? What's the rush, Burke? Are you going back to Chicago?"

"Eventually."

"It's a cliché to say this is so sudden, but— This is so sudden. Why?"

His face took on a stubborn expression, not unlike his son when he didn't get what he wanted, when he wanted it and under the terms he requested.

"Why not?" he answered. "Think about what you'd have."

This was beginning to sound like a business deal and a chill started in her stomach then spread slowly outward. "Spell it out for me."

"First, there's a big house. Cars. I know you'd like that." He thought for a moment. "You talked about traveling to some place warm in the winter."

"Wow."

"Hawaii. Florida." He completely missed the underwhelming tone in her voice so when he went on she didn't interrupt. "Tahiti would work. Would you like to scuba dive? There's a reef on a small island in Micronesia that's supposed to be the best in the world for seeing manta rays." He looked at her. "Have you been to Europe?"

"No."

"I could take you there. It's spectacular. London. Paris. Rome. Venice. Florence. We could lease a private yacht and see them all."

"And the only catch is that I have to marry you."

His brows drew together. Frustration or annoyance? It wasn't clear. "I can take you away from all this…"

She remembered the night he'd surprised her with flowers and dinner. Such a romantic gesture it took her breath away. But it was also the night when he'd said he would never marry again. Followed by the statement that the only commitment he could make was to do what was best for his son.

This was a decent proposal, but it was coming from a place where it was best for Liam, which meant it would never work in the long term.

"If that's your best offer, you don't know me at all."

There was a flash of something in his eyes and this time it was clearly anger. "We could be good together. You. Me. Liam—"

"No thank you, Burke."

"Syd, think about this—"

"It's probably best if you go now."

Since she was so easy to read, Syd turned away before he could see the expression in her eyes that would be a giveaway about how hard it was to turn him down. Without another word he left and she was alone. Alone with the realization that she'd said no because she was in love with him. Hell of a time to realize the truth of her feelings.

Now she understood why she'd been on the defensive when he made his case for marriage. He'd skipped the most important step.

The one where he told her he loved her.

Chapter Fourteen

Syd was in no mood for a family get-together, but a girl didn't always get what she wanted. Thoughts of Burke Holden immediately came to mind along with the scene of his proposal here in her home just the day before. If she'd gotten her wish, he'd have asked her to marry him as if he really meant it. Not because she was his solution to a child-care problem.

Now she was standing in the kitchen with her dad, Loretta Goodson beside him, her brothers and their families gathered around the big, granite-topped island. They were all waiting.

Her father put his arm around the waist of the woman standing next to him. "I have an announcement to make."

"You're pregnant," Ben joked.

His pretty blonde wife, Camille, stared at him in mock horror. "You're a doctor. Remarks like that could start rumors that you skipped anatomy class."

"I've heard that rumor." His older brother, Alex, elbowed him. "There's another one currently circulating that he patched up a broken leg with Super Glue."

"Why don't you guys just stuff a sock in it and let Dad speak," Syd snapped. "Your daughters are more mature than you. I'd call you two-year-olds, but that would be an insult to toddlers."

"Wow." Alex looked at her, one eyebrow raised in surprise. "Someone got up on the wrong side of the bed today."

"That better not be a remark about this being that time of the month." Even as Syd's anger shot into the stratosphere, she knew it was misplaced. Alex wasn't the man she wanted to verbally eviscerate.

"Why don't y'all quiet down and hear what your dad has to say." There was something peacemakerish in Ellie McKnight's soothing Texas drawl. "And Alex, my love, apologize to your sister for that insensitive remark."

"Whatever you want, sweetheart." Alex leaned over and kissed his wife's cheek. "Syd, I'm sorry you're irritable and surly."

"And I'm sorry you're a male chauvinist pig." Somehow she managed to keep her tone teasing and everyone laughed.

"Okay, if you're all finished?" Tom looked around expectantly and everyone nodded. There were no more smart-aleck remarks. He took a deep breath. "I asked Loretta to marry me and she said yes."

There was a moment of silence while the information sank in. No one was really surprised; they'd all known this was coming. And when the hush ended, whistles and words of congratulations started. It was clear that everyone approved. Then there was a lot of hugging and kissing.

Syd did her best to hide her romantic trouble. How ironic that her dalliance with Burke had started because of her determination to convince her dad he could and should move on with his life. The romantic pretense hadn't lasted long because she and Burke had a genuine connection and they never had to work at it. At least for her it was effortless. Her dad just made the announcement about getting married again and Syd couldn't let him know that she and Burke were not now—and never would be—a couple.

She looked around at her family. Her dad and his fiancée tenderly touching and kissing. Alex and Ellie, her arm through his, talking intimately. Ben swinging Cam into his arms for an impromptu dance around the kitchen. Her two little nieces exploring the only cupboard not child-proofed, pulling out the kid-friendly stuff inside as if they were getting away with something. It was crowded, loud, chaotic.

Syd had never felt more alone in her life.

If she didn't do something her dad would see there was a problem. "We need the right kind of liquor for a special toast. I'll run into town and see if I can get some champagne."

"Not necessary." Her father put a hand on her shoulder to stop her from leaving. "I stashed a couple of bottles in the garage refrigerator."

"Then I'll go get it," she offered.

"Let me," Alex said. "You round up some glasses."

"Okay."

Too bad. A couple minutes in the solitude of the garage might have helped with an attitude adjustment. She'd been willing to go the extra mile to get her dad right where he was and didn't want to spoil this lovely memory with her bad mood. It was tough to be hearty when your heart was broken.

"We don't have champagne glasses," she informed them. "Not even the plastic kind from New Year's Eve. Although it will offend my sister-in-law the hotel heiress's five-star sensibilities, I think wineglasses will work. I *propose* we do that."

As intended, there were loud groans at her pun. Cam wrinkled her nose at the idea of champagne in the improper glass but conceded it was the best option. That didn't stop her from mumbling about a little warning and she could have arranged to borrow the right flutes from the lodge.

Ellie and Cam pitched in to help so that when Alex returned and popped the cork on the bottle, an eclectic group of glasses waited on the kitchen island. Seven to be exact. An odd number. Because Syd didn't have anyone.

As her vision blurred with tears, she was nudged aside while her brother poured the bubbly golden liquid. Then the glasses were handed out. The toddler girls got sippy cups with juice even though they were too little to understand what was happening around them.

"As the eldest son, I propose a toast," Alex said. "To Dad and Loretta. Congratulations!"

Everyone sipped.

Then Ben cleared his throat. "As the second son, an heir and a spare," he said, "way to go, Dad. Welcome to the family, Loretta."

Loretta's eyes were suspiciously moist. "Thank you. That means a lot to me. It was important to Tom that you all approve, so I'm glad you do."

"It was never Alex and Ben who worried me."

Syd couldn't meet her father's gaze. He'd said something similar just before Burke had driven into the auto shop for the first time. The pain of that memory sliced clear to her soul and somehow she had to keep them all from seeing. It was her turn to propose a toast.

"Ben and Alex have memories of Dad with Mom, but I don't. To me there was always sadness in his eyes. Until Loretta." She held up her glass. "To the woman who put a twinkle in my father's eyes. Thank you for making him smile again."

Loretta hugged her, too moved to speak. There was a chorus of "aww" and then everyone drank.

When the excitement died down, the conversation turned to wedding plans. "This is going to be a short engagement. A week, maybe two," her father said. "Just long enough to put together a simple ceremony at the church. Family and friends."

"That would be pretty much the whole town of Blackwater Lake," Alex pointed out.

"And we wouldn't have it any other way." Loretta smiled up at the man she clearly adored. "As the mayor of this town, I have resources."

"And she knows how to use them," Tom said proudly. "This woman can delegate. But we're going to need everyone's help."

"Anything you need, Dad." Syd meant that with all her heart. After all, she'd propositioned a perfect stranger in order to move her father's romance along.

"I was hoping you'd say that." Loretta met her gaze. "Because I'd like you to be my maid of honor."

Syd's chest tightened as she reached out to hug the woman who would marry her father. "It would be my... honor."

"Cam, Ellie, will you be co-matrons of honor?"

"Of course," they both said at the same time.

While everyone was oohing and aahing over the engagement ring, Syd slipped quietly out the back door. She drew in a deep breath as the chill in the air cooled her face. The only light was what spilled from the kitchen. She'd never felt so much like she was on the outside with her nose pressed up against the window, wishing she had what everyone else did.

Finally all by herself, the tears she'd been fighting trickled down her cheeks. Her chest hurt from holding everything back and the realization dawned that in all her life she'd never been quite this miserable before.

She never heard the back door open, but suddenly strong arms came around her and pulled her into a comforting hug. Her father's familiar warmth wrapped around her.

"What's wrong, baby?"

The kindness and support just made her cry harder, but her dad silently held on until the sobs quieted.

"Oh, Daddy, you should go back in. I didn't want to spoil the celebration."

"You're not spoiling anything."

"I tried not to let anyone see how upset I am."

"You're my girl." He sighed. "I know you too well. When you snapped at Alex for making a joke, it was a dead giveaway. Usually you're the one leading the smart-aleck attack. You can't hide how you feel from your old man. Consider that a warning."

"Understood."

"Now," he said, snuggling her a little closer, "tell me who made you cry."

"Burke." She sniffled. "He asked me to marry him."

Tom gave her one last quick, hard hug before putting her away from him. Light from the window underscored his puzzled expression. "I'm sure there's a connection between the crying and the proposal, but for the life of me I can't figure it out. Do you want me to take him out back and beat the tar out of him because he *wants* to marry you?"

"Of course not." She took a shuddering breath. "He told me once that he would never marry again. His wife was a selfish witch who doesn't want to be a wife and mother."

"I'd say he chose poorly, but—"

She held up her hand. "And he also said that every decision he makes is based on what's best for his son. So the fact that he asked me to marry him really has nothing to do with me. With us."

"How can you be so sure?"

"He never said he loved me—" An emotional lump in her throat blocked the rest of her words.

"I warned you not to get hurt, but I guess that's not something you can help." Tom shook his head. "I'm really sorry, honey. It's likely you learned to be wary of love from me. And you should know that your mom would be very put out with me for teaching you that."

"You didn't. It goes way back to when Charlie and Violet eloped." She'd vowed not to get hurt again. The circumstances were different, but the result was the same. Her heart was crushed.

"The message your mom would stress is to take life in both hands and live every day as if it were your last." He gently tapped her nose. "That's what you made me see when you concocted that ridiculous scheme to make me think you'd met the man you were going to marry."

"Ironically he did ask. Even though it backfired on me, I stand by my decision to make you see that it's okay to be happy."

"I appreciate that more than you'll ever know."

She brushed away a tear that was rolling down her cheek. "I was afraid if you knew about Burke and me you'd call off the wedding. You're not, are you?"

Her dad shook his head. "That wouldn't fit with my new philosophy. I just want you to be as happy as I am."

"I will be." She gave him a quick hug. "And I want you to know that I don't need a man. I have my family and I know you guys are there for me."

"Absolutely." He glanced over his shoulder. "I have to get back. Do you need another minute by yourself?"

"Yeah. Thanks for understanding, Dad."

"Anytime."

After her meltdown at being the only single McKnight, Syd better understood her father's desire to see her settled. It seemed that for her, settled meant being by herself. What she'd had with Charlie wasn't a deep and lasting emotion; Burke had shown her the difference. She was in love with him and knew that losing him would hurt for the rest of her life.

As with her father, there would always be a sadness in her eyes.

Burke sat alone in a booth at the Grizzly Bear Diner and contemplated his half-eaten Papa Bear burger. The combo wasn't quite as appealing or exciting as the first time he'd ordered it, but everything had changed since then.

Liam was living with him, although tonight he was having dinner with his friend Todd. Burke had taken Syd to bed for amazingly nice sex. More important, the first Papa Bear burger experience had been before Syd fixed a hamburger for him at her house.

He was realizing that it was the company, not the food, that made everything taste better. And if the look on her face the last time he'd seen her was anything to go by, Burke wouldn't be getting another invitation to dinner at her house.

Maybe that was for the best. He'd hurt her and didn't want to do it again.

From his booth in the back he saw Mayor Goodson walk into the diner alone. She stopped at the hostess podium and chatted with Michelle Crawford, the diner owner, who was filling in for Violet Stewart. The two ladies were looking very serious about something, then the mayor smiled and lifted her left hand while Michelle thoroughly examined one of the fingers. The appraisal was followed by a hug.

Burke guessed that Loretta was showing off an engagement ring. If he was right, and he would put money on it,

Tom McKnight had popped the question and his proposal had been accepted.

If Syd was here they could share a high five. Mission accomplished. But she wasn't here. Apparently Loretta was going to be, though. Michelle pointed in his direction and the mayor walked resolutely toward him.

"Hi, Burke."

When she sat down across from him he decided they were apparently going to have a conversation.

He nodded. "Madam Mayor."

"How are you?"

"Fine." He looked at the diamond on her left ring finger. "It would appear that congratulations are in order."

"Tom asked me to marry him." She extended the hand and looked dreamily at the tangible proof of the engagement as if she still couldn't believe it was real. "We told the kids last night."

By "the kids," he was pretty sure she was referring to Alex, Ben and Syd, who had to be ecstatic about this turn of events. Her dad was finally moving forward with his life. If Burke had played any small part in the successful outcome, he was pleased. He would have been more pleased if Syd had personally passed along the news. He missed her.

It had only been a couple of days, but he craved the sight of her.

"How did 'the kids' take the announcement?"

"They were all very happy for their dad. And me," she added.

Don't say it, he warned himself, but the words came out anyway. "How's Syd?"

"She was the most pleased for her father." The mayor's eyes narrowed. "Because she felt responsible for him hesitating on the proposal."

"Right." Not a news flash and not what he really wanted to know.

"In fact she was afraid her dad would call it off when he found out the two of you were over."

"You know?"

"In this town good news travels fast. Bad news spreads at light speed." She shook her head and gave him a pitying look. "Poorly played, Burke. I expected better of a hotshot like yourself."

"I'm not sure what you mean."

"You're not seriously going to make me spell out the pitfalls of what happened, are you?"

"I asked her to marry me," he protested.

"And listed the perks as if a proposal was a job interview." Loretta actually tsked. "And there were no flowers, dinner or grand gestures. This conversation happened just inside the door of her house. While you paced like a caged tiger. A very unhappy one."

"Whatever happened to 'it's the thought that counts'?"

"That's the thing. It didn't sound like you thought it through. Along with the houses, cars and trips, you offered to take her away from all this." She held out her hands, a gesture that included all of Blackwater Lake. "Did it occur to you that she might not want to leave? That someday she'll be taking over the business Tom spent his life building? That she loves this town and it's in her blood?"

No, he hadn't thought about that. But it was a confession he had no intention of sharing. He was a man of action. The business wouldn't have exploded under his leadership if he'd been anything less than that. But apparently when dealing with women, being a man of action had its drawbacks.

As far as he could see, there was only one fallback position here. "I was sincere about wanting her to marry me."

"Really?" There was no anger, frustration or sarcasm

in her tone. Just pity. "You wanted her to marry you. But do you want to marry her?"

"I asked, didn't I?"

"It was the way you asked." She leaned forward, resting her forearms on the table between them. "As if you wanted her to say no."

A man of action never wanted rejection. Now he was starting to get irritated. "How did Tom propose to you? What did he say to get a yes?"

Her look was wry. "He certainly didn't leave out the three most important words. In fact, he led with them."

He knew what she was saying. Those three words were all that stood between him and another failure. "It was a decent proposal."

"Was? You're giving up?"

"What am I supposed to do? She turned me down flat and said don't darken her doorway again."

"She actually said that?" The mayor's tone was skeptical.

He shrugged. "It was more like don't let the door hit you in the backside on the way out."

"Can't say I blame her."

This woman was an expert at sending mixed messages. First he was giving up and now she was validating Syd's reaction. "Whose side are you on?"

"That implies you expect special treatment because of the business your development project will bring to Blackwater Lake."

Sydney was the only thing on his mind and if he could change that he would do it in a heartbeat. "Believe it or not," he said, "I wasn't thinking about business at all."

"I'll have to trust you on that, Burke. And trust me when I say that I'm not taking sides. Both of you are my concern."

"Okay." He met her gaze. "I suppose everyone in town knows about this?"

The mayor smiled. "A person in this town would have to be living under a rock not to. But everyone likes you and wants the best for you and Syd."

"Glad to hear it." If he focused hard enough on Liam and the job he came here to do, maybe he wouldn't miss Syd so much.

"I have to go meet Tom. And for the record he doesn't know I talked to you. I just stopped by to show Michelle my ring and she mentioned you were here."

"So you decided to read me the riot act?"

"That wasn't the riot act. Believe me, you'd know if it was." She met his gaze. "But I'm asking a favor. I'd like you to think about something."

"Okay."

"You don't strike me as the sort of man who gives up easily. It seems out of character."

She was right about that. He was also smart enough to know when not giving up turned into beating your head against the wall.

"Syd made her feelings clear," he said.

"Did she? I wonder. But that's for you to decide. This is my 'buck up' speech." She cleared her throat. "I've been in love with Tom for a number of years now, long before he was ready to move on from losing his wife. If I'd given up, I wouldn't be getting a happy ending now."

"So that's the message? Don't give up?"

"We only fail when we fail to try," she said. "For what it's worth, folks in Blackwater Lake are pulling for you and Syd."

"Why?" he asked skeptically.

"You're good people. And she's one of our own. We want you both to be happy." She slid out of the booth and stood. "Okay. That's all I have to say and worth what you paid for it."

"Thanks, Loretta. I appreciate you talking to me." Then he remembered the question that she'd skirted before. "How's Syd?"

She sighed and there was sympathy written all over her face. "She's as miserable as you."

That information should have given him some satisfaction, but it didn't.

Chapter Fifteen

Burke was sitting on the sofa watching a movie with Liam. On the flat-screen TV stuff was exploding and giant robots were morphing into cars, trucks and helicopters. It was loud and didn't require much concentration. That was fortunate since he couldn't concentrate, at least not on this.

All he could think about was Sydney and the void in his life now that she was gone.

Liam missed her, too. It had been over a week since they'd spent time with her and the boy had been asking questions. When were they going to see Syd? Could they go to her house for dinner? Maybe she and Burke could sit on the patio again while he practiced with his new soccer ball.

Burke was running out of excuses. Pretty soon he was going to have to tell his son that they wouldn't be seeing her anymore. And he knew why he was putting off that conversation. Saying the words out loud would make it final and that was going to hurt like hell.

There was a knock on the door and he looked at his watch. Eight at night was kind of late for a visitor. But he felt a small spurt of hope that maybe Syd had had a change of heart.

"I'll see who's there."

Liam looked at him. "Do you want me to pause the movie?"

"No, that's okay." He didn't know what was going on now and missing a minute to answer the door wouldn't make much difference.

He walked across the suite and looked through the peephole, but Sydney wasn't standing there. It was his father and for some reason that surprised him more.

He unlocked the door and opened it. "Dad. What are you doing here?"

"Granddad!" The TV sound stopped when Liam paused the movie, then ran over to greet the newcomer. "I didn't know you were coming."

"That makes two of us. What's up, Dad?"

"Do you mind if I come inside for a few minutes?"

So he wasn't planning on staying long. Burke figured that was standard operating procedure for his father.

Liam grabbed the older man's hand and tugged him into the suite. "I'm so glad you're here. Aren't you glad to see him, Dad?" The boy looked up and frowned. "You don't look happy."

It was more about not trusting than anything else, he thought. Walker Holden only showed up when it suited him, so there had to be a reason he was here.

"If I'd known you were coming, I'd have picked you up at the airport." He met his father's gaze.

"I rented a car. I'll be very happy when you and Sloan get this resort project going and build an airport close by. It's nearly a hundred miles from the current one."

None of that explained the reason for this visit. Burke

figured he wouldn't know until his dad was ready to say what he wanted.

"Can I get you a drink?"

The other man nodded. "Scotch if you have it."

"Of course."

Burke had cultivated a taste for good Scotch because he knew that was Walker's favorite. It would be something they had in common. Maybe a bond. But that was many years and a lot of crushed expectations ago. He'd finally faced the fact that he would never be at the top of his father's priority list.

Burke walked over to the bar, where several kinds of liquor and glasses were arranged. He took two tumblers and poured a small amount of the amber liquid into each.

"Can I have a soda?" Liam's look was pleading. "You and Granddad are going to toast to something and I need something to drink, too."

"Okay. But nothing with caffeine. You have school tomorrow and it's almost bedtime."

"But Granddad is here. Can't I stay up a little later? It's a special occasion."

Burke knew how he felt. As a kid on those rare occasions when his father had been home it had been special for him, too. "Maybe a few minutes—"

"But, Dad, I don't get to see him a lot now that we don't live in Chicago."

Reading between the lines he would have to guess that at home the two had seen each other frequently. When had Burke missed that?

"I'll be here for a while, Liam. We'll spend a lot of time together."

"O-okay," the boy said grudgingly.

Clearly the old man was uncharacteristically patient and understanding. Even diplomatic. When did that happen?

As soon as everyone had their respective liquid, Liam said, "I think we should drink to Granddad's visit."

"Okay." Burke clinked his glass with theirs. "Where are you staying, Dad?"

"Here at the lodge. But I couldn't get a suite on such short notice."

"When did you decide to come?" Burke thought a round of twenty questions might shed some light on the mystery.

"Two days ago. After using Skype with Liam." He sat on the sofa with his grandson beside him and an arm around the boy's shoulders.

Burke sat across from them. They made an affectionate picture and he had an odd sensation that felt a lot like envy. He didn't remember sitting with his father like that. It was hard to do when the man was gone all the time.

"So, what did you two talk about on Skype?"

"You." His father sipped his Scotch. "How unhappy you are."

Burke looked at his son's expression that was just this side of guilty. "Liam?"

"It's true, Dad. You don't smile. You don't want to play ball. And when I ask if we can go to Syd's house your mouth gets all weird and your eyes are mad. Did Syd do something?"

She said no, he thought, and was taken aback by the way his chest got tight at the memory. More pressing, though, was the fact that the conversation with his son about her absence from their lives was going to happen much sooner than he'd expected.

"Syd didn't do anything," he said.

"Then you must have done something." His father's voice was neutral, not critical or harsh. Just matter-of-fact.

Still, Burke felt defensive. "Why does it have to be my fault?"

"Because that young woman is sensible, practical and straightforward. Salt of the earth. Pretty, too. I like her."

"I don't need your approval." But Burke was annoyed that he still couldn't stop wanting it.

"Your mother would have liked her, too." It was as if the man hadn't heard his son push back. "Sydney reminds me a lot of your mother."

Liam leaned closer to his grandfather. "I wish I could have met her."

"You would have loved her."

There was a tone in the older man's voice, a wistful sadness. And the look in his eyes was an echo of the expression that had been there right after his mom had died. It was a mixture of fear and pain. Burke recognized it because he'd felt the same way.

"I'm sorry you never knew her, Liam." Burke sipped his Scotch and waited for the burn in his throat to subside. "She was sweet and funny. She taught me to be kind, loyal and loving. That's who she was."

"I didn't deserve her," Walker said.

Burke stared at the man who was acting nothing like his father and wondered where the heartless bastard had gone. "Why do you say that?"

Instead of answering he looked at his grandson and smiled proudly at him. "More than anything I'm sorry that your grandmother never knew you. She would have loved you so much and been so proud of you, Liam. You too are kind, loyal and loving. Your father instilled in you all the qualities that his mother made sure he had. Everything he needed to be a good father he learned from her. Not me."

"Dad?" Burke stared at the man whose voice and face were familiar, but the attitude was something new.

His father's eyes were bleak. "I should have been around more after she died. I'm sorry I wasn't. You're raising a terrific young man. In spite of my bad example, you're a wonderful father."

Liam smiled up at him, then looked at Burke. "Yeah. You're pretty cool, but way cooler when Syd's around. Maybe you should apologize to her for what you did."

"First, I think we should hear what he did to alienate the young lady."

"Syd's not young," Liam said.

"She is to me," his grandfather pointed out.

"Why does everyone assume it's my fault?" The two just stared at him and Burke sighed. "Okay. All I did was ask her to marry me."

"Well done." Then his father's smile faded. "Yet the two of you are estranged."

"Dad's not strange." Liam looked confused. "Syd isn't, either."

"It means they're not together," Walker explained. "When Sloan and I were here, I saw for myself that she cares very deeply for you. It surprises me that she didn't accept your proposal."

Burke figured he might as well confess and move on. Maybe even change the subject. "I told her about all the perks of being married to me."

"You mean like a job interview."

That's what the mayor had said to him. Had he actually proposed to her in a way designed to make her refuse?

"Yeah, it was pretty much like that." Burke got up and moved to the bar to pour himself another drink.

His father stood and followed him. Behind them the TV sound came on, meaning Liam had lost interest in the men's conversation.

"Burke, I know I wasn't a very good father to you and I'm sorry. There's something about having a grandchild that makes a man examine the mistakes he's made and try to do better. I can never undo what happened or make it up to you. There's no reason you should hear me out now, except that I'm asking you to."

Burke figured there was nothing left to lose. "Okay, I'm listening."

"When your mom got sick I wanted to fix it because that's what I do. But this was out of my hands and I felt helpless. Then she died and I didn't know what to do with the pain. I had everything money can buy and lost the one thing it couldn't. Love. The day your mother was buried was the day I buried myself in work. I'm very sorry I wasn't there for you, son."

Burke just nodded because there was a lump in his throat the size of Montana.

"I can't help thinking that you learned to run from love and that I'm the one who taught you to do it."

"My ex-wife gets some of the credit."

"Pinhead." His father's voice dripped with loathing. "I knew she was wrong for you, but didn't say anything. Figured you wouldn't listen to me of all people. There's no place in hell low enough for a woman like that."

They both glanced at Liam, who was intently watching the movie and paying no attention to this conversation.

Burke blew out a long breath. "He stopped asking about her a long time ago. But I'm sure at some point he'll want information."

"When he's old enough to handle it, you and I will be there to help him deal with the repercussions." His dad reached out and squeezed his shoulder. "And I hope Sydney will be there with you, son. I didn't say anything to you regarding my doubts about your first marriage. Whether you listen to me or not I won't make that same mistake now. Don't follow in my footsteps and isolate yourself from the people who care about you."

Burke felt years of resentment slip away. "Why did you come all the way to Blackwater Lake, Dad?"

"Because I love you and Liam. In the event that you needed me, I wanted to be here to help."

Burke knew he wasn't just talking about Syd, but everything that happened after his mom died. He could have sworn there was a cracking sound in his chest followed by ice falling away from his heart. His father was warning him that love was everything. If Burke lost the woman he loved while there was a chance of having her, he would turn into a bitter shell of a man.

He pulled his father into a hug and felt the heaviness he'd carried for so long lift from his shoulders. "Thanks, Dad."

"Thank you, son." They stepped away and looked at each other and his father said, "Now, what are you going to do about Sydney?"

"That's a good question."

It was amazing how fast a wedding could be pulled together when the whole town pitched in to help. As promised, Loretta had mobilized and delegated, starting a phone tree to spread the word about when and where, and that the reception would be a potluck in the church multipurpose room right after the ceremony at the church located in Blackwater Lake's town square.

Syd's dad had asked her Uncle John to be his best man while her brothers would be groomsmen. Flowers were ordered, nothing extravagant, just simple and beautiful.

Now Syd stood in the back of the church. Double doors separated this area from the rows of pews. As instructed, she was wearing her favorite dress—a red number with a peplum that hugged her like a second skin and four-inch heels to match. Her heart hurt terribly, but she had to put that aside because nothing was going to spoil her father's big day.

Still, she thought that Liam might have liked to be here.

Then she pictured his eager little freckled face that was so much like his father's. Once was a fluke. Twice was a pattern. It seemed that when she gave away her heart, she lost not one, but two people she cared about.

Fortunately, just then her two sisters-in-law joined her. Cam was wearing a royal blue dress with a draped bodice showing a hint of cleavage. Ellie had on a green number with long sleeves and a flirty skirt. The jewel-toned shade highlighted her beautiful eyes.

Syd looked them over and smiled. "You both look completely stunning."

"Are you sure?" Cam smoothed the front of her dress with the hand not holding a bouquet of white roses and baby's breath. "In my wild heiress days, I was in charge of fundraising and fashion events where a designer's career could be made or marred forever. I even walked the runway on occasion. But I've never been this nervous."

"No one would mistake me for the fashion police," Syd said. "But in my humble opinion you look fantastic. You, too, Ellie."

"That's a relief," she said, her Texas roots strong in her voice. "Alex told me that, but everyone knows we dress for other women and he's a man." Her eyes twinkled. "And then he tried to get me out of this dress."

"*Very* high praise." Cam looked Syd up and down. "I've never seen you look more amazing. Burke Holden is my friend, but he's a complete idiot. He doesn't know what he's missing. I tried to talk to him and make him understand that you two are made for each other, but he's being stubborn and—" The words stopped when Ellie cleared her throat. Cam looked mortified. "I'm so sorry. Me and my big mouth."

Syd desperately wanted to ask for specifics about what he'd said, but this wasn't the time. She had the rest of her life to wonder why he couldn't love her. "It's okay."

"No. I'm usually more sensitive than that, but I guess today I'm more nervous than sensitive."

"Don't worry about it." Syd did her best to smile and hoped she pulled it off. "I'm great. Where do you two have my nieces stashed?"

"Maggie Potter has Amanda," Cam said. "Her mom, brother and his fiancé are watching Leah. So, with Maggie's little girl, Danielle, four adults are keeping track of three toddlers. But the little ones usually play nice and keep each other occupied."

"Okay, then." Syd nodded. "Whatever will be will be and that's how Dad and Loretta want it."

"Did I hear my name?" The mayor had emerged from a room off to the side that was reserved for brides. She was wearing a cream-colored lace-over-silk tea-length dress with a neutral shade high heel.

"You look beautiful," Syd said. "Are you nervous?"

"No. I can't wait to be Mrs. Tom McKnight."

As if that was her signal, Rinda Bartell walked over. The blue-eyed blonde was a church volunteer who coordinated weddings. "We're ready to start, ladies. The gentlemen have taken their places in the front with Pastor Will. Sydney, you'll be last before the bride. Camille and Ellie, who wants to go first?"

"I will," Ellie offered and Cam gave her a grateful look. "One of the first things I did here in Blackwater Lake was break my ankle so everyone knows I'm a klutz. If I fall today, Cam, just go around me. I'll be a distraction. That should take care of your nerves."

"It doesn't," she said. "But let's do this."

"I'll go cue the organist," Rinda said and hurried away.

They had a moment for wishes of happiness before Ellie opened the doors separating the rear of the church from the pews. Then the music started and she headed up the aisle.

Cam waited a few beats then followed. Syd gave Loretta a thumbs-up gesture before starting her walk.

People filled the seats and the ones on the end that she could see smiled broadly and murmured that she looked beautiful. Diane and Norm Schurr gave her a little wave. Jill and Adam Stone, with their son and daughter, were there. She passed Violet, Charlie and their kids. This time she grinned at them and meant it. Finding happiness wasn't easy and she was glad for her friends.

She saw her father with Uncle John beside him. Her brothers were there, too, and all the men looked incredibly handsome in their dark suits. Just before she took her place, her gaze settled on her dad. He nodded his approval, then his expression changed. He looked expectant, or excited. She knew him as well as he knew her and this was something more than a man about to get married.

Before she could wonder what was going on, his expression changed, filled with happiness, and she knew he'd seen his bride walking toward him. Her father took two steps to meet Loretta and held out his arm. She put her hand in the bend of his elbow and they moved in front of the pastor.

"Tom, Loretta, in front of most everyone in Blackwater Lake I have to say—it's about darn time."

The congregation laughed, including the bride and groom, dissipating any lingering nerves. Then the pastor cleared his throat and started the ceremony. "We are gathered here today in the sight of God, family and friends to join Tom McKnight and Loretta Goodson in marriage."

He talked about love being patient, kind and understanding. The obligations of a husband to his wife and vice versa. Her father and Loretta vowed to love, honor and cherish then exchanged rings. The minister said the "I now pronounce you husband and wife" part and it was time for him to announce you may kiss your bride. But that's not what he said.

"Ladies and gentlemen, there's someone here who has requested permission from Tom and Loretta to say a few words."

Syd heard the click of a man's shoes walking down the aisle and glanced in that direction. Her legs started to tremble when she recognized Burke and Liam Holden approaching. The boy looked so handsome and grown up in his suit and tie. And Burke... Seeing him was like a shot of adrenaline to her system. She couldn't believe he was here.

He stopped in front of the wedding party and thanked both the pastor and her father. After that, all his attention was focused on her.

"Syd, you were absolutely right to refuse my proposal. It was decent enough, but not even close to what you deserve. I can do better. Please hear me out."

"I will," she whispered.

He moved closer, stopping about a foot away. When he spoke, his words were clear and loud enough to be heard in the church's far corners. That was partly because in spite of the capacity crowd, it was possible to hear a pin drop.

"When I asked you to marry me, I said I would take you away from all this. It was glib, a cliché. The truth is that Blackwater Lake is part of who you are and I would never change you. I love you and that means never asking you to choose between me and what you care so deeply about. But I'd move heaven and earth for you. That includes my corporate office. I plan to set it up here in Blackwater Lake."

Syd had the ridiculous thought that she hoped whoever her father had asked to video the wedding was still recording because she would want to see it later. Burke was still talking and she was pretty sure it was important but all she could focus on was the "I love you" part.

Then he said, "You would make me the happiest man in the world if you'd marry me."

Before she could even process those words and form a response, Liam spoke. "I love you, too, Syd. And I want you to be my mom."

That's when the tears she'd been struggling to hold back trickled down her cheeks. And judging by some loud sniffling and a chorus of "ohs" she wasn't alone.

She glanced at her father, who stood with an arm around his new bride. "You knew about this?"

"Burke asked for my permission to propose. I gave it without hesitation. He's a good man. He'll take very good care of my little girl."

"Oh, Daddy—" Her voice broke.

And then Burke was holding her and whispered against her hair, "Please don't cry. I wouldn't have crashed the wedding if he hadn't been on board with this."

She nodded. "But why was it so important to do it here? Why now?"

"For one thing I needed a grand gesture." The corners of his mouth turned up. "But it's more than that. Your father's happiness is as important to you as yours is to him. As he takes this step forward in his life, it was necessary for him and everyone in Blackwater Lake to know that I promise to love and protect you as long as I live."

"Oh, Burke. That's so—"

"Please don't say nice." He smiled. "Just say you'll marry me."

"Since that's a much better proposal than the one I made to you—yes." She pulled back just enough to see his face and said in a voice as loud and clear as his had been, "I love you, too. Of course I'll marry you. There's nothing I want more than to be your wife and Liam's mom."

There was spontaneous applause and when everyone settled down, the pastor cleared his throat. "Now it gives me great pleasure to say—I present to you, Mr. and Mrs. McKnight. Tom, you may kiss your bride." His grin was wide when he said, "Burke, you may kiss your fiancée."

Burke didn't waste any time. He cupped her cheek in his hand and smiled tenderly before touching his mouth to hers. She sighed with happiness and felt a soft puff of air on her face, like the caress of a mother's fingers or the brush of an angel's wings.

Suddenly awareness filled her heart and soul that two mothers who couldn't be here in body for their children were here in spirit and signaling their approval of a most decent proposal.

* * * * *

Available April 21, 2015

#2401 NOT QUITE MARRIED
The Bravos of Justice Creek • by Christine Rimmer
After a fling with Dalton Ames on an idyllic island, Clara Bravo wound up pregnant. She never told Dalton the truth, since the recently divorced hunk insisted he wasn't interested in a relationship. But when Dalton discovers Clara's secret, he's determined to create a forever-after with the Bravo beauty and their baby...no matter how much she protests!

#2402 MY FAIR FORTUNE
The Fortunes of Texas: Cowboy Country
by Nancy Robards Thompson
On the outside, PR guru Brodie Fortune Hayes is the perfect British gentleman. But on the inside, he's not as polished as he seems. When Brodie is hired to fix up the image of Horseback Hollow's Cowboy Country theme park, one lovely Texan—his former fling Caitlyn Moore—might just be the woman who can open his heart after all!

#2403 A FOREVER KIND OF FAMILY
Those Engaging Garretts! • by Brenda Harlen
Daddy. That's one role Ryan Garrett never thought he'd occupy...until his friend's death left him with custody of a fourteen-month-old. He definitely didn't count on gorgeous Harper Ross stepping in to help with little Oliver. As they butt heads and sparks fly, another Garrett bachelor finds the love of a lifetime!

#2404 FOLLOWING DOCTOR'S ORDERS
Texas Rescue • by Caro Carson
Dr. Brooke Brown has devoted her entire life to her career—but that doesn't mean she isn't susceptible to playboy firefighter Zach Bishop's smoldering good looks. A fling soon turns into so much more, but Brooke's tragic past and Zach's newly discovered future might stand in the way of the family they've always wanted.

#2405 FROM BEST FRIEND TO BRIDE
The St. Johns of Stonerock • by Jules Bennett
Police chief Cameron St. John has always loved his best friend, Megan Richards—and not just in a platonic way. But there's too much baggage for friendship to turn into romance, so Cameron sets his feelings aside...until Megan's life is threatened by her dangerous brother. Then Cameron will stop at nothing to protect her—and ensure their future together.

#2406 HIS PREGNANT TEXAS SWEETHEART
Peach Leaf, Texas • by Amy Woods
Katie Bloom has fallen on hard times. She's pregnant and alone, and the museum where she works is going out of business. Now Ryan Ford, the one who got away, walks into a local eatery, tempting her with his soulful good looks. Ryan's got secrets, but can he put Katie and her child above everything else to create a lifelong love?

YOU CAN FIND MORE INFORMATION ON UPCOMING HARLEQUIN® TITLES, FREE EXCERPTS AND MORE AT WWW.HARLEQUIN.COM.

HSECNM0415

When Harper had gone back to work a few days after the funeral, Ryan had offered to be the one to get up in the night with Oliver so that she could sleep through. It wasn't his fault that she heard every sound that emanated from Oliver's room, across the hall from her own.

Thankfully, she worked behind the scenes at *Coffee Time with Caroline*, Charisma's most popular morning news show, so the dark circles under her eyes weren't as much a problem as the fog that seemed to have enveloped her brain. And that fog was definitely a problem.

"Do you want me to get him a drink?" she asked as Ryan zipped up Oliver's sleeper.

"I can manage," he assured her. "Go get some sleep."

Just as she decided that she would, Oliver—now clean and dry—stretched his arms out toward her. "Up."

Ryan deftly scooped him up in one arm. "I've got you, buddy."

The little boy shook his head, reaching for Harper.

"Up."

"Harper has to go night-night, just like you," Ryan said.

"Up," Oliver insisted.

Ryan looked at her questioningly.

She shrugged. "I've got breasts."

She'd spoken automatically, her brain apparently stuck somewhere between asleep and awake, without regard to whom she was addressing or how he might respond.

Of course, his response was predictably male—his gaze dropped to her chest and his lips curved in a slow and sexy smile. "Yeah—I'm aware of that."

Her cheeks burned as her traitorous nipples tightened beneath the thin cotton of her ribbed tank top in response to his perusal, practically begging for his attention. She lifted her arms to reach for the baby, and to cover up her breasts. "I only meant that he prefers a softer chest to snuggle against."

"Can't blame him for that," Ryan agreed, transferring the little boy to her.

Oliver immediately dropped his head onto her shoulder and dipped a hand down the front of her top to rest on the slope of her breast.

"The kid's got some slick moves," Ryan noted.

Harper felt her cheeks burning again as she moved over to the chair and settled in to rock the baby.

Fall in love with A FOREVER KIND OF FAMILY
by Brenda Harlen, available May 2015 wherever
Harlequin® Special Edition books and ebooks are sold.

www.Harlequin.com

Love the Harlequin book you just read?

Your opinion matters.

Review this book on your favorite
book site, review site, blog or your own
social media properties and share
your opinion with other readers!

HARLEQUIN®

A *Romance* FOR EVERY MOOD™

JUST CAN'T GET ENOUGH?

Join our social communities
and talk to us online.

You will have access to the latest
news on upcoming titles and special
promotions, but most importantly,
you can talk to other fans about your
favorite Harlequin reads.

Harlequin.com/Community

 Facebook.com/HarlequinBooks

 Twitter.com/HarlequinBooks

Pinterest.com/HarlequinBooks

HSOCIAL

THE WORLD IS BETTER WITH

Romance

Harlequin has everything from contemporary, passionate and heartwarming to suspenseful and inspirational stories.

Whatever your mood, we have a romance just for you!